CRIMSON FOG

For My Beloved

CRIMSON FOG

SHATTERED SOUL

R. B. RIOS

iUniverse, Inc.
Bloomington

CRIMSON FOG
SHATTERED SOUL

This is a work of fiction. All of the characters, names, incidents, organizations, and dialogue in this novel are either the products of the author's imagination or are used fictitiously.

iUniverse books may be ordered through booksellers or by contacting:

iUniverse
1663 Liberty Drive
Bloomington, IN 47403
www.iuniverse.com
1-800-Authors (1-800-288-4677)

Because of the dynamic nature of the Internet, any web addresses or links contained in this book may have changed since publication and may no longer be valid. The views expressed in this work are solely those of the author and do not necessarily reflect the views of the publisher, and the publisher hereby disclaims any responsibility for them.

Any people depicted in stock imagery provided by Thinkstock are models, and such images are being used for illustrative purposes only.
Certain stock imagery © Thinkstock.

ISBN: 978-1-4620-4604-1 (sc)
ISBN: 978-1-4620-4605-8 (ebk)

Library of Congress Control Number: 2011915958

Printed in the United States of America

iUniverse rev. date: 08/29/2011

Prelude

"When you have forever, who do you choose?"

Chapter One

Fleeing The Nightmares

The bright light blazed on my skin, as I writhed from the immense pain. I could feel the fire and deep itch coursing through my veins as I tried to gasp for air! I was clawing at my throat trying to breathe. My lungs were choking from the lack of oxygen and they burned so badly as if on fire. I tried to scream but no sound came from my too tight and raw swollen throat. Well no legible sound anyway. My head threatened to burst from the terrible throbbing that made my skull too small for my pulsating grey matter, my eyes burned from how dry they were as they bulged from my sockets. I couldn't focus on anything as the whole environment around me spun out of control and I couldn't tell which way was up.

My fingers dug at my throat again, at my sides, my flailing arms, at the floor and at the empty air above me as I tried to ease the burning itch that I just couldn't get too. I heard my name being whispered in a sing-song manner in my ear. "Kee-kee-oh . . . Kee-kee-oh . . . Kikyo!" Then I finally found my voice. I screamed. No, it was more like I shrieked! I shrieked from the pain when my lungs found enough air to fill them. I shrieked until I saw or think I saw a shadow move from the corner of my burning eyes and I was so frightened. I could smell something vaguely familiar, heavy and metallic in the air that filled my nostrils with its scent was it lightening? It was familiar but I couldn't make it out. I heard a sound wailing in the background and it sounded as if I should recognize it but incomprehension filled my head as the sound escalated becoming louder and clearer, then I realized that the sound was *me!*

I awoke with a startled jolt that sent me crashing from my bed to the hardwood floor with a thud as I smacked my head against the bedside table! I was tangled in the sheets and couldn't focus my eyes at first. My chest was heaving, and I was sucking in ragged breaths of air. I turned my head to read the clock through blood and tear blurred eyes, As if I really had to. I knew all to well that it was 3 am. Just like every day for the past four months. What did this mean? I hugged myself tight trying to hold myself together until the shaking eased some and I could untangle the sheets from my body. No use trying to sleep anymore tonight, I knew *that* would be a huge impossibility. I got up on unsteady legs and went down the darkened hallway to the bathroom, as I flicked on the too bright light I resisted the urge to look in the mirror. No use looking if I already knew what would look back at me. I quickly splashed some cold water over my face, cleaned the newest head wound just above my hairline, brushed my teeth, and finger combed my hair into a poor excuse for a pony tail. The cool water felt good over my feverish skin. Television had never really held my interest at this hour, I used it mainly for background noise, and anyway I preferred to do something less lethargic than watching infomercials. I needed to burn off some adrenaline.

Still shaky, I got dressed in an old pair of joggers a tee-shirt and my running shoes. I was never big on running before but I figured this was all I could do to keep from going insane. I grabbed my light track jacket from the hook by the door and did a mental checklist to make sure I had all I needed. I packed my key and i-Pod into my pocket, pulled on the ear buds glanced at the time (3:30) and grabbed the door knob behind me. I kicked away the morning newspaper that I never read, but always forgot to cancel.

The early morning air carried a chill as it was still late April. It was a clear pre-dawn morning, and I could see some of the brighter stars up in the heavens. I stepped out onto the front porch and locked the door behind me. I took a quick uneasy look around my neighborhood, and saw what I saw every day. The usual Chicago inner city, gang activity was in full swing as I took a deep breath and crossed myself. This was not the best of neighborhoods for me to go running in (unless I was running for my life).

My house stood in the direct center of the block. It was a bungalow style house. I lived on the first floor with the full basement, and I had a vacant apartment on the second floor, but somehow I wasn't ready to rent it out. The house to the left belonged to a nice elderly woman who lived with her divorced son and his children; the house to the right was the typical neighborhood crack house, the gang leaders' house and the whore house all in one. At the end of the block was a huge apartment building which I had never had a reason to go into, thank goodness because it always creeped me out.

I shuddered to myself as the eyes of the guard standing in front of the door to the crack house leered at me. I took the steps from the porch in three strides, running to the sidewalk in front of my house. It was difficult to decide which way to go if I went north on Cortland towards St. Louis that was one Gang's territory, but if I went south to Kimball that was a different territory. Either way was not a sensible choice. I picked up the volume on my, i-Pod tucked my head down and began to jog towards North Ave. by way of Kimball. I jogged until I reached North Avenue and turned East with the only possible destination in sight. My destination for the past four months was Humboldt Park a few blocks from my house. All the while I felt cold eyes follow me as I took off.

This had been going on for some time now, you'd think that my silent watchful "neighbors" would be used to me running at this hour, alone. But I put them out of my mind as I tucked my head down even tighter and took flight. I didn't look back for fear of meeting those eyes that seemed a little *too* focused on me. I realized that I was a little more than just jittery; I was down-right scared! I figured it was safer for me to take my chances with the street than with my insanity in my own big lonely dark house. I was more terrified of what lurked in my imagination and the dark shadows of my house than of the gangs and the night life in the streets. Out here they could kill me quickly if they so chose. Inside I was being slowly driven insane.

I ran until I reached the far edge of Humboldt Park, on California Avenue turning the corner to go south to reach Division, then West onto Kedzie Street and back down to North Ave. again. When I had successfully circled the park's perimeter, I decided to head home. I could feel the terror beginning to build in me when I had to go back to my house and face another day of loneliness, and isolation. But this is not what had me uneasy. I had a *feeling* that I was being watched or followed or possibly watched *and* followed. There was a strangely familiar scent in the air that I couldn't quite make out. My head swam with possible places I could run to for cover as the uneasiness quickly built up in me, but at this hour nothing was open and the only people around were of the unsavory kind. I had to get out of here as fast as possible.

The hair on the back of neck stood on end and the adrenaline raced through my entire body, giving me the strength to take flight and really run. I raced home never looking over shoulder, and rarely stopping for a breath. I avoided looking anywhere but down. I got back to my front door, fumbled with the key in the lock and flung myself in as soon as the door unlocked. I was panicked but why? I turned all the latches on the door to secure it and finally remembered to breath. My hands were shaking as I took off my jacket and turned off the i-Pod. I was more wound-up now than when I first left.

I let out a very tense sigh of relief that I was home. Safe at home, strange that now I felt safe, when the reason for my running was the exact opposite of safe. I knew this was silly of me. There was no one out there with me. No one followed me and no one was out to get me. The house stood empty except for me. It was dark and silent like a tomb, like my heart.

I quickly undressed in the darkness of my room and went to shower in the tiny bathroom. I caught a glimpse of myself in the door length mirror hanging behind the door and what I saw startled me! I was covered in scratches and scars from neck to knee and I had a wild look in my eyes. The scratches were a result of my nightmares, my only companions for the past four months. I turned on the hot water in hopes of relaxing my too tense and too tired body, cringing from the sting on my new open wounds as I stood in the hot steamy stream of water. I sank slowly into the filling tub, and hugged my knees to my chest as I finally let go and cried. I cried for the total loneliness that consumed me.

I cried for the loss of my beloved mother who had died six months ago. I cried for the loss of my innocent youth that gave way to instant maturity when mom was diagnosed with breast cancer and gone in less than a month. I cried because I had pushed everyone in my life away except my mom over four years ago not fully knowing why, and now I was utterly alone. But most of all I just cried. I cried until I was light headed and all cried out. I cried until my lungs ached from the heaving sobs, I cried until I was empty inside once again. All the pain now gone replaced by a calming numbness that was equivalent to a dream state.

I had never given myself permission to cry because I had to be strong. I was a loner in this world and I was only 17, a senior in high school and declared an adult when mom . . . departed. It was so unfair! I, like mom was an only child. She had been orphaned in Durango, Mexico when she was only 4 years old. She was passed from relative to relative that didn't want and couldn't afford the burden of another mouth to feed. She left the little village when she was thirteen and made her way to the coastal touristy city of Huatulco to make a better life for herself. Mom was living on the streets of the city for about four years. She sold gum, candy and trinkets to the tourists in the plazas and had even learned enough English from the tourists to sell her livlyhood.

Mom instantly fell in love with and married my dad Hiro Aoki, a week after meeting him when he was on spring break vacation from college with some friends in Huatulco. Mom was head over heels in love with Hiro Aoki who was twenty three, and on a work study visa from Japan. And according to mom totally gorgeous he spoke enough Spanish to vacation with and have a whirlwind romance with. Mom was only seventeen, but smart, streetwise and beautiful. He loved her just as instantly and promised her the moon and the stars. They married in a small church in Huatulco a week after meeting. She came to the U.S. blissfully content to begin a life with her new husband and leave the only life she knew behind.

I was conceived during their short courtship. Mom was exstatic about her new life only to have her husband my father, die in the crossfire of a gang related drive-by shooting almost eight months after their wedding. The shock of losing Hiro was too much for her and I came earlier than expected, mom was only seven months pregnant when I arrived into the world on October 18, 1991 weighing in at 4lbs. and 5oz. and at 12" in length. Mom thought she would lose not only her new husband, but her child as well. I pulled through, and as sickly as I was, I eventually was strong enough to go home with her and start our lives together. She never gave up though. She always told me that I was her world, her reason for living. And that I was the reason she was born. My dad had invested most of his savings (which he had gotten when his parents passed away in his sophomore year of college) into filing for mom's residency, so we were not very well off. We had lived in hotel rooms, mom's friend's houses, and small one bedroom rat and roach infested apartments.

But my mom was resilient. She had two jobs, leaving me with friends she had made while she worked. Mom learned better English, eventually filed for citizenship, raised me on her own, and never complained about it. When she had saved enough money for a house, she found one in the only place she could afford. The house was cheap because of the neighborhood it was in, but none-the-less it was our house. Mom furnished it with second hand and dumpster furniture.

I was not allowed outside for obvious reasons and no one was allowed inside either, unless she was home, which was rare because she still had two jobs even then. It didn't matter though because I was never good at being friends with anyone. I was so shy and self-conscience because of my physical traits that I didn't truly fit in with any group. I didn't look totally Mexican or Asian; I was a mix of the two. I was rail thin and shorter than average for my age. My hair was black, long and wavy; my eyes sort of oval with very long lashes and my skin was an off shade of light tan.

The only friend I had was a boy named Tristian, who was my age and the son of my mom's co-worker and best friend. When you spend enough time on your own, you tend to guard your isolation.

Señora Garcia was married to a half Caucasian half Mexican man named Tristian Jr. who was an alcoholic; he took his drunken rage out on her and Tristian III, when he bothered to come home at all. But she was always available to help mom watch me, whenever we needed her. So Tristian and I were all we had really, besides both our moms.

That was all so long ago, I met Tristian way back in third grade, and he was the only one who never made fun of me, or tried to bully me. He was the only person in school who defended me when I was too shy to defend myself. Tristian went out of his way to make sure I was ok and fought for me many times; he was my only real friend. I hadn't really thought about Tristian much since the beginning of freshman year. I had pushed everyone away from me in the beginning including Tristian. He had tried calling, and coming over but I couldn't stand to be around him, and I didn't know quite why.

Life went on for me through high school uneventfully. It was always just mom and me, while she worked, I went to school, and when she wasn't home, I studied alone. I missed my mom everyday. When mom passed away she took with her my desire to live. Sure I still went to school I was a senior now and I worked at a small hot dog stand a few blocks away on Armitage. I didn't really have a life or expenses, so the money I had earned was all sitting in a bank account that was rarely used, except for bills. And I had thought to myself then . . . I can survive this. Along with the house mom left me some money not a lot but enough to cover funeral expenses and have a little left over to add to my college fund. If I went to college at all I knew it would be community college, it was all I could afford and all I could tolerate.

I broke out of my reverie when I realized that I was shivering, the water had run icy cold. Just how long did I sit in the tub I wondered? I quickly got out and got dressed. I wasn't working today and it was Saturday. I went to the little kitchen and debated if I was hungry or not. I opted for not. I shut the fridge door and went to sit at the dining room table to do some homework. I still couldn't shake the feeling that someone was watching me, but I chided myself for being silly and dug into a report I had to write on "Of Mice and Men". It wasn't due until a few weeks for my final, but I had nothing better to do. I tried to focus my attention on the report but that nagging feeling wouldn't go away.

I gave up on homework and did housework instead. I had a pile of laundry that had to be done, but going into that basement always creeped me out. I would toss the pile of clothes in my arms down the stairs and race down. Turn on every light I passed, shove the laundry into the washer pour the detergent, start the machine and fly back up in a matter of minutes. I picked up a rag and began to dust from top to bottom, and room to room. Well all rooms except of course mom's I still hadn't allowed myself the agony I knew it would bring to go in there. Maybe soon I would be strong enough to go in there. I needed to get some papers in order, and get rid of her clothes, and things she was no longer in need of.

I had to run downstairs to throw the clothes into the drier, and as quickly as I had it into the washer it was in the drier. I glanced around the basement and shied away from the ominous look of the ancient furnace that always reminded me of a giant octopus. The house was old, and the furnace once upon a time used to burn coal, but had long since been converted to natural gas. I thought I saw a flicker of movement in a shadowy corner, but quickly released that thought and took flight up the stairs before tripping up the stairs, only I would be capeable of tripping *up* instead of down. I cussed under my breath, and rubbed the already forming bruise on my right shin. Great what was one more bruise?

There was one room in that basement that I was terrified of, but I had no clue as to why. The previous owners had left it completely stocked with building materials, and tools. Just to be near it in the basement, sent chills through me, and made my heart race, so I stayed away as much as possible.

I was actually getting hungry now and realized that it was almost noon. I made a quick sandwich and laughed bitterly to myself as I was on my way to the living room to turn on the television mainly for background noise and to not feel so alone, when I could hear a memory of mom telling me to use a plate and sit at the table. I listened. I ate and let my mind wander. I daydreamed about being in a big family with lots of brothers and sisters and lots of cousins, aunts, uncles and grandparents. Not my pathetic one person family. One person did not make up a family. It was strange how everyone in my life was an only child, mom, dad, me and even Tristian. I mused at the thought that I was truly utterly alone in this world. If something happened to me, who would know? Who would care? I heard the buzzing of the drier and went down one last time to get my clean clothes. I didn't bother to look around; I just grabbed everything and escaped the basement, yet again as I quickly turned off all the lights.

Once I had put away my clean clothes, put away my school work, and put away the feeling of uneasiness, I wanted nothing more than to sleep. I was exhausted, not from my mundane chores but from the lack of sleep. I somehow couldn't remember my nightmare, because when it was daylight out it was hard to make sense of the foggy fragments left in my brain. I had to sleep, really sleep in order to become somewhat normal again. My eyes had dark purple bruises under them and I was more frail than usual. I normally ate only when I realized that my stomach was crying out for nourishment so I was essentially a zombie. I hardly even spoke anymore unless I was asked a direct question from my boss, a customer or one of my teachers.

When was the last time I had a real conversation with a person I wondered. Maybe I needed professional help. But that was just too out there for me. What could I possibly learn from a shrink that I didn't already know myself? I was lonely, I was grieving, and I was just so depressed. Maybe I needed medication? Maybe I should medicate myself? The crack house *was* just next-door. No I could never do that! I could never take pills or smoke anything or stick needles into my arms. What would mom think about that? Unacceptable! Why was I even thinking that? What was wrong with me? Why was I so abnormal? Why were there so many questions in my life and no one to ask for answers? They say everything happens for a reason, but what possible reason was there for the way my life had turned out? If only my mom were still around even if she didn't have all the answers I needed at least she could hold me tight and kiss away my fears.

I had to get out and clear my head. I had to go anywhere that was not here or the park. I needed to be with people, not just my thoughts. I checked my wallet to see how much money I had and realized that I hadn't even been to the bank in about a month, I had about three uncashed checks in my wallet but I did have enough cash for a movie. What was playing I wondered? I hadn't a clue, as I rarely even turned on the television, and the radio hadn't been used since mom died. My only company was my i-Pod and my thoughts.

The closest movie theater around was Logan Theater but I somehow had a bad feeling about that one, that neighborhood was as bad as mine. So I figured on going to the western suburbs to a nice theater in Melrose Park, a suburb of Chicago. I grabbed the car keys (mom passed her beat-up old "Brady Bunch-ish" station wagon to me as well) and locked up the house. I hated going into the ally but the wagon was in the garage and I needed an out as fast as I could get it. I checked the gas gauge and saw I still had almost a full tank. I usually just walked to work and took the good old Chicago city bus to school.

I felt this was going to be good for me. It's been ages since I was out to see a movie. Mom and I would rent movies on occasion, mostly monster movies those were her favorites. But the last time I went to a Movie Theater was also a lesson to me that I wasn't to be trusted around people. I was so out of place. I went once in freshman year with a group of school classmates that I couldn't even call friends. It was my first attempt after my accident to get back to semi-normalcy and make friends. I went with them to this very theater and I had no clue as to what to do with the boy who sat by me and constantly fired question after question at me about my life. Why didn't I have a boyfriend? Why didn't I have any girlfriends? Why didn't I have *friends* in general? Why didn't I ever talk to anyone? Why was I always alone? But the weirdest question was about my wardrobe, why did I always were turtlenecks or sweaters no matter the weather? He even said that I was trying to be Goth, but wasn't really pulling it off, even though I had the Emo thing going but not the attitude. Finally I had enough of the boy and had to leave but since we all came as a group we had to leave as a group, so I sat in the lobby until the movie was over and I was the first stop on the drop off list even though they did go out of the way to get me home first. What a disaster that was. Needless to say those classmates went out of their way to avoid me from then on.

I always talked to mom in English and she always talked to me in Spanish, just so that the other could always be practicing the second language. "I guess I wasn't very good company huh?" I asked mom when I was home way too early, and way too depressed. "Kikyo, honey, why do you let them bother you? Make an effort to be friendlier, you don't even talk to Tristian anymore, call him, and go out with him. He was such a good friend to you, and you push him away, aw honey what am I going to do with you?" Mom had encouraged me to go with the group that consisted of four girls, and five boys. The boy who had sat next to me, for some odd reason wanted to befriend me, and poor guy, I guess I was the exact opposite of what he was expecting. Again I asked . . . what was wrong with me? Only mom would understand me. Only mom would care enough to kiss me and make everything all right. Only mom could or would love me unconditionally.

But that was all past me now. I drove slowly out of the city limits into the suburbs. I drove west on North Ave. until I found my way past my neighborhood, past Pulaski Street, past Harlem Ave. and as I passed "Kiddie Land" a children's amusement park, I knew 9th Ave. was just a few blocks away. I drove into the vast parking lot found a spot far in the back and didn't even bother to lock my wagon, who would want it?

I walked up to the ticket booth and asked for a ticket to any movie that was about to start or had recently started. The girl behind the glass looked at me with a bored expression on her face and passed me a ticket and some change. I didn't even know what I was going to see. Was it a comedy, a horror flick, or a romance? At this point I didn't really care. To my surprise it was a blood bath, filled with monsters, and epic fights. It was a good change to see something not in my head full of foggy memories. I actually had a good time, it reminded me of mom. Granted I was alone but at least I was out of the house and doing something for a change. I figured that since this was an occasion to celebrate (being among the living) and it was still early, I would head home and maybe even call the closest person I had to a friend. I wondered if Tristian still considered me a friend. I wondered if he would even take my call. But maybe he didn't have plans and wouldn't mind coming over to keep me company for a while. I had been thinking about Tristian all day. What was I thinking? This was not the usual *me*. But I had to do it before I talked myself out of it. I fished my address book out of my wallet and found his number. I went to the first available unoccupied phone I saw and dialed.

"Um Hi", I stumbled and paused after I realized that I hadn't spoken to Sra. Garcia since mom's funeral. Sra. Garcia spoke English well but always insisted that everyone speak to her in English so that she can constantly practice. It was also her way of helping my mom with her own English. "Sra. Garcia, how are you? I hope your well. I know I haven't called in so long, and I'm sorry. I hope Sr. Garcia is well. Is Tristian home by any chance?" I was so nervous that I was sure I sounded like I felt. "Kikyo, hija what a surprise, how are you dear? Is everything alright? I do hope so. Tristian is right here, I'll get him for you. Please come by and visit dear, we miss you so much. If you need anything, please just call us and we'll do what we can. Here's Tristian, take care of yourself hijita, bye."

"Hello?" said the smooth incredulous voice of Tristian. "Kikyo, is that you? Geeze what a surprise! How have you been? Are you ok? What's wrong? Geeze I haven't talked to you since . . . since . . . ." His voice trailed off as he realized that the last time we spoke was at mom's funeral. "Sorry 'bout that" he said sheepishly. "What's up?" I took a deep breath, "Tristian I was wondering" (I was never good at this sort of thing) "Tristian are you busy tonight?" I paused hoping he wasn't doing anything. I really needed company. "Um well I *was* going to go out with some friends tonight you wanna come along?" "Um no thanks that's ok, you go ahead. Maybe we can do something some other time then." My heart sank a bit at the prospect of an empty house yet again. "No, no, don't be silly, I can go with them anytime, do *you* want to do something I'd really like to see you again."

A deep blush crept to my cheeks, and spread all over my body. I shuddered at what I must've looked like to the people milling about the lobby. I was nervous as we made arrangements to meet at my house in an hour, watch a movie and call out for a pizza. I raced home, and I don't really know what I was so on-edge about but I just couldn't sit still as I watched the clock waiting for Tristian to get to my house. We had briefly "dated" for a while in grade school, and he was the only person who knew me as the person I was before high school, when I was still semi-normal.

I was a little startled when the doorbell rang, and ran to door catching a glimpse of myself in the hall mirror. As a rule to myself I avoided mirrors, I had such an aversion to seeing what I looked like, I don't truly know why, but I guess I never really felt pretty, let alone beautiful. And the scars were ever present, sometimes on my face, but mostly on my arms and neck. I was a mess! I tried to smooth out my hair and put a smile on my face. For the first time in a little over 3 months I actually had someone in my house besides my imaginary moving shadows. I flung open the door with a little too much enthusiasm, and a wide grin was plastered on my face mirroring the same look on Tristian's face. "Come in, come in" I said as I stepped away from the door. As soon as he stepped in, he shut the door behind him, and I awkwardly hugged him. We went into the living room and waited for the food to arrive.

I hadn't actually seen Tristian in a long time and at the funeral I was so out of it that I barely noticed him, but looking at him now, I wondered when the boy I knew in grade school grew up to be the man he was now. Tristian had long straight chocolate brown hair, which he kept, tied in a ponytail with a leather band. He had the most perfect mustache and goatee, his eyes were the same chocolate brown as his hair, and his lips were naturally red and slightly pouty, kind of like mine and he also had impossibly long eyelashes, and he towered over me by almost a foot.

Tristian was an athlete in school and was in excellent shape. Wow I mused when did my friend turn into *this* I wondered with a slight blush.

Tristian quickly filled the uncomfortable silence with endless questions about how I was doing, what I've been doing. Had I been accepted to any college, what my plans were, and so on? I was grateful for the company but a little sad because I hadn't the slightest idea what to talk about. I still didn't know what to do after graduation. I had honestly not given any thought to my future. I knew mom would want me to go to college in the Chicago area and even if I went away, what difference did it make? It's not like I had anyone here to stay for. Or any desire to really go away either. I had never given any thought as to what my career would be. All I ever really had any interest in was trying to figure out my past, but it was so foggy. I chewed on my right thumb nail, lost in concentration, and slowly heard a murmur that pulled me back to earth. Tristian was shaking my shoulder, not roughly but enough to get my attention.

I came back to reality, and smiled sheepishly at Tristian. "Sorry 'bout that I'm not really used to actually having someone to talk to, or should I say talk to me back." I could see the worry in his eyes for me. "We *used* to be so close Kikyo, what happened to us?" all I could do was look down at my lap, where I kept wringing my hands together over and over. "Are you ok? Do you need anything?" Suddenly I was not so sure this was a good idea. Maybe it was too soon for me to be around anyone yet. But I didn't want to hurt his feelings, so I put on my *day* face. A mask of contentment that I'm sure really didn't convince anyone. "No, Tristian I'm fine, look it's just that (I stammered for the right words) it's just that I still miss mom that's all"

He was about to argue with me about my obvious off-truth, when the doorbell rang, with the pizza delivery man. Tristian jumped up quickly to get the door, as I was left to compose myself, and silently scold myself for inviting him here where I'm sure I was making him uncomfortable. But to my surprise, he smiled at me over the pizza box he carried to the coffee table, and gave me a wink so sweet that tears threatened to well up in my eyes. "Hey didn't you promise me a movie? What are we watching?" I shooed the dark clouds that had invaded my soul away, and tried to be the girl I was in grade school, that girl I knew was still in me somewhere.

I popped in the first tape I found, not looking at the title. We settled-in and as the movie started, each of us on a corner of the couch. Tristian was very comfortable, and acted like our four year separation had never occurred. I drifted off to sleep, not realizing that as I did I snuggled closer to him, and he wrapped one arm around me. I came-to and to my embarrassment; he was smiling down at me. The horror! "Wow if I knew that I was *that* boring I wouldn't have come" I knew he was teasing, but I felt awful for falling asleep on him anyway. "I'm so sorry! I didn't mean to do that!" He was looking at me then with a serious expression, one of concern. My eyes darted away from him, wanting to hide the ghosts of my nightmares from my eyes. I knew that if he truly looked into my eyes that he would see into my soul, and if what awaited me behind my very eyes frightened me, what would it do to him?

"Geeze, Kikyo, when was the last time you had a good nights sleep? Your eyes are red and swollen, and you have so much baggage under them, that you can carry steam trunks! Is it school? Is it work?" I didn't really want to talk about my nightmares, and I definitely would not tell him about running alone at night. So I lied, was this the beginning of so many more lies to come? "Oh Tristian, you know I have to work. I have to go to school, and study. I have to save enough to go to college, even if it is community college. I'm not sure what to do about *that* just yet, maybe I'll take a year off, and sort out my plans. You know mom didn't exactly leave me well off. Yes the house is paid for as well as the wagon, but there are always bills and taxes. What else can I do?" The ever present budding tears began to well up in my eyes, but I refused to let them fall. I blinked them back and cleared my throat. I was a little embarrassed to see that he was still cradling me, and when he saw me blush, he let me go. We both stretched, and when we realized the time, it was already, Tristian got up to help me clean so that he could go home.

When we were done, I was more comfortable, and I was glad that I had broken through that wall of loneliness even if it was for one day. Tomorrow would be a better day I promised myself. I gave Tristian a quick hug, and he promised to call, and made me promise to call as well. Even though he was only going to the end of my block where he parked, I felt like I needed to protect him somehow from our "neighbors" as he walked to his car. Silly me, like if *I* could really do anything against the gangs if they decided to pick on him. But I was worried for Tristian. And this was good, not only because I had someone to worry about, but because I even *cared* enough to worry. What a strange life I led. I watched him drive away, and felt a sense that changes were in the air. For better or worse I hadn't a clue, but change was good, and I was ready.

Even though I slept during my visit with Tristian, I was exhausted. He was right, I was very weary looking. I sighed in defeat, and got ready for bed. Even before mom died, I was never really popular, or had many friends. I always felt a little on the outside. I usually had my nose stuck in a book either for school, or just enjoyment. I was forever walking around dazed, and more than a little confused. No wonder I didn't have any real friends, everyone thought I was some kind of freak; even the freaks at school avoided me. But after mom passed away, it only got worse. I was so introverted that I think I actually was a zombie! I would hear the snickering of the girls behind my back; I would hear the boys talking about me also saying things like I was weird or strange. No one understood why I was like I was, geeze even I didn't fully understand it. But I wasn't in any major hurry to fix it. The way I was made people leave me alone. I didn't fit in, never had. All my clothes were either black or dark and boring, my hair hung limp and lifeless in my face, I was pale and never wore make up, so my bloodshot eyes, had purple circles under them but my lips however carried a natural scarlet hue to them.

Mom had tried to tell me time and again that I had to try to get along. I had to try to make friends. I had to try forgetting the past. I never knew what she was talking about, what past? What past did I need to forget and why? Every time she said it, she refused to say what exactly I was supposed to forget, so I tried even harder to remember usually giving myself a migraine in the process. The only person in my entire high school who tolerated me was of course Tristian he's the only one who would defend me although I don't know why because since freshman year, I shut out the world; I shut down myself but most of all I shut out Tristian. It was like I couldn't trust people, but especially boys. When they tried to get close even if in distance I stiffened up and after a while they all just avoided me. When mom died it only got worse. And now I had sort of began my ascent from this dark pit of confusion and despair I kept myself in. it was a long climb out but I had to try. I had to get out before it was too late and there was no permanent escape for me.

Chapter Two

Emergence

With a stifling scream, I awoke again from the same dream, from the same sense of danger and horror. All I remembered of the nightmare was the scent again, and "Kikyo . . ." being whispered over and over in my ear. My throat was raw and swollen again from my screaming. How long exactly *had* I been screaming? I wondered if my neighbors could hear me. Maybe the sweet old lady next door or her son heard me screaming night after horrific night. Could someone across the street hear me, or even God-Forbid, my neighbors to the right? Why wasn't someone banging on my door? Why wasn't someone calling the cops? Not that the cops even came to *this* neighborhood, until the damage was already done, and it was too late. I was heaving, and sobbing. My face was sweat and tear streaked, my arms bleeding from where I had re-opened the healing scratches form every other night. I shot a nervous glance at the clock again 3am. When would this end, soon, never? I went through my daily motions as I had for the past 4 months. I dressed, and went for my daily early morning run. I was so tired. I was so weary. And all I could think was why? Why was I suffering like this? What was the point? Mom died; get over it I scolded myself. Moms died everyday, just like dads, brothers, sisters, and whole families.

Why was this so hard for me to accept? I stepped out of the house once again, and caught the eyes of the guard standing in front of the door, to the house to my right. He never said anything, only stared at me. He was a big guy, like an old football player. He was bald, tough, and menacing and extremely tattooed and pierced. He stood guard just like every other night, his huge muscular arms crossed in front of his massive chest, just staring. I took off in my same pattern towards Humboldt Park, just like everyday. Why did I have to live like this? Why was I so freakishly abnormal? I ran in my usual pattern, but couldn't escape the feeling that again someone was behind me, or to the side of me. No, that wasn't right. It was as if someone was *around* me like everywhere at once. But again . . . why? I headed home after going around the park, and caught a split second of a glimpse of someone in the shadows watching me. And I hurried home where I slammed the door shut after I flew through it, and fell on my knees, my head in my hands, and stifled a sob. My whole body vibrated with the adrenaline rushing through my body. I was hyperventilating and wheezing. I muffled my dry sobs in my hands, and let the tears cloud my vision but not fall.

Once I got control of myself, I went to the bathroom and ran a hot bath; maybe a bubble bath would relax me, and untie the mass of knots that were my muscles. I was wound up so tight, that at first I couldn't even feel the hot water; I only knew it was hot because it turned my skin red, and I could see the steam rising from my body. I hugged my knees to myself and rocked until I finally quit shaking. Should I call the cops? No. what good would that do? I stayed in the water until I was a prune. The bubbles had dissolved and the water became icy cold. I was soar from being in the same position for so long. It was Sunday and I didn't have to work today either, strange, but for some reason I found that comforting. I knew that sleep was not coming anytime soon. I got out of the tub, and wrapped a towel around me tightly, and pulled a brush through my wet hair. I brushed my teeth and felt somewhat normal for an instant. I stepped out of the little bathroom, and stood frozen as a shadow moved in a corner of the living room ceiling. Was I seeing things? What did I think I saw? My knees turned to jelly, and blackness surrounded me as I fell into a dark abyss, complete with images that made no sense, and scents that were familiar, but indefinable.

I woke up with the sun blaring on my eyelids; hazy thoughts were in my head. I was stiff from lying on the floor for so long without moving. Suddenly I remembered why I was on the floor in the door way between the kitchen and the dining room. As I got up my eyes darted from side to side, sweeping the length of my house and finding nothing. Not a spec of dust out of place. Was I dreaming? Was I seeing things now? I was shaking again, but I could sense that I was alone in my house. I got dressed, and decided I had to go somewhere. I couldn't stay here all day. I had to get out, even if it was to sit in the wagon in the garage the remainder of the day. I just couldn't be in the house. It was already 5:00 pm and I had school tomorrow.

I was on my way to my room again to get a horror book to read while I sat in my car for the rest of day, when the doorbell rang, sharp and shrill, it shook me to my core. Who on earth could be at my door? I honestly had no idea. I considered not answering it, but I peeked out from behind the drapes and let out a breath I didn't realize I was holding when I saw that it was Tristian! Just as he was about to turn and leave I flung the door open and he whipped around to see the grin on my face. His went from worry and panic to elation in a fraction of a second. He quickly stepped into my hallway, and gave me a bear hug. He swung me off my feet, and his eyes twinkled in the joy of seeing my mask of glee. But this took me off guard, I had just seen him only yesterday, why was he so happy?

"Kikyo, why on earth didn't you answer the phone? I was worried sick! I've been trying to get you since I got home Saturday night. When you didn't answer I got worried, but thought maybe you turned the ringer off at night. And then Sunday, I tried you again, and again, and again. I thought maybe you went to work, so I looked for you there and they told me you had the day off. But then, when you didn't go to school Monday or today, I *had* to get over here and if it meant coming back with the useless cops, I would. But I was just about to brake in your door, if you hadn't suddenly opened it. Kikyo Starlita Aoki Martinez, don't you EVER scare me like that again you got it?" He was mad at me? I couldn't fathom why. He said I didn't go to school today or Monday, but today was Sunday, not Tuesday, was I right?

When realization hit me over what he'd said, I looked at him confused, more than confused, I was down right bewildered. Just how long was I out? He was looking at me with deep concern. And all I could do was stare back at him with the most idiotic expression on my face. My head started to throb. And it was like a memory was trying to break through. What *was it*? It was like I could almost make it out, but that memory was smoke and the more I tried to grasp it, the more it dissipated. I had to sit. My vision was blurred, and my head wanted to split in two! Tristian could see the worry on my face, except it wasn't worry, it was terror! I took a deep breath and led him to the living room couch as we were still standing in the hallway. I was trying to rationalize why I had woken on the floor two days later, this didn't make any sense. Why did my foggy memory have to be so flimsy!

"Tristian, I honestly don't know what's going on with me lately." I said to him, and his brows knit in concentration. "Are you sure it's Tuesday?" I asked again incredulous, but not really thinking he'd make it up. "I think I'm losing it, I'm cracking up!" I was starting to shake, and he put his arms around me. "I can't sleep, I keep having recurring nightmares, I wake up at exactly 3 am every day, and I just don't know what's wrong with me!" I think I was hysterical at this point because the shock in his eyes calmed me down some. "Look I *think* I keep seeing shadows, I think I'm being watched, and know in my core that I'm definitely being followed. But I don't know for sure. I'm not sure of anything. My head is so confused, so foggy. I think it must be like some post grieving stress disorder if there is such a thing." He hugged me tight and kept whispering that everything was going to be alright. He stroked my hair, and rocked me slightly in his safe strong arms.

I really did feel safe in those arms. But maybe it was just a reaction to my lack of familiarity, I wasn't used to being held like this. But it was so comforting, I wanted him to *never* let go. "Let me call my mom and see if you can stay at my house. It's no wonder your falling apart your in this house all alone! For God's sake Kikyo your *only* 17! You live alone, you don't socialize, you work, you study, and what? What do you do for company? Why haven't you called me? Why did you push me away? I hate to see you like this. It's my own fault really, I should have checked on you; I should have busted down your door, or cornered you in the halls at school. But you were always inside some kind of protective bubble! Why did you lock me out?" I lowered my eyes and honestly had no answer.

I stared at him choosing my words wisely; I didn't want to scare him away from me. I liked Tristian, he was my only friend in the whole world, and I didn't want to hurt him. But I didn't want to give him false hopes that I could give him anything in return. I was like an empty shell. I was so tormented by memories that refused to materialize in my mind, and horrible nightmares that were driving me insane. But I couldn't find the right words to truly explain my misery. So I told the truth, or as much as I believed was truth anyway, even if he thought I was berserk.

We sat on the couch, and he saw the sadness in my eyes. Tristian took my shaking hand in his, and held it tight. He traced circles over the palm of my hand with his thumb, and let me ramble, always knowing when to nod, and "uh-huh'. "Tristian, I've never been a real "people" person, you know that. It's hard for me to talk to people let alone grant them access into my own personal bubble. But with you it's always been so easy. I like that our mom's forced us together at first. It feels like so long ago. It feels like a lifetime ago. You've always been there for me, only you. How strange that you're the only person on this planet who I can talk to and not feel that I'm making a fool of myself, or that I'm just some freak or something." He squeezed my hand then to confirm what I'd just said. He didn't want to distract me. I continued. "All through grade school, when everyone picked on me for being slow, or too quiet, or too shy, or too anything, you always stood up for me. And when we started high school, I was truly horrified at the thought that you might get bored being my babysitter, and not want to be around me. So before I could allow that, I started to shut you out, slowly of course so it wouldn't hurt so much for either of us. I pushed you far enough away until you were just another classmate, just another face in the crowd. It was so lonely without you. The girls were always being terrible to me. They would talk about me like if I wasn't even there. They all said that I was weird, or mental, or something along those lines. But it was worse with the boys because they all seemed to agree that I was a freak. So I built my bubble and locked myself in it. I could see that all my teachers felt bad for me. But what could they do? So I just built up walls around my heart and mind so that it wouldn't hurt so badly.

Tristian had the saddest expression on his face, and wiped a tear from my eye. I hadn't even realized that I was crying. I bet he would leave here tonight and never come back. What a head-case I was. He squeezed my hands again and nodded to me to continue. Why was he being so nice to me, I wondered? "Go on Kikyo, please I want to know" he encouraged me. "The summer before freshman year, something happened to me. I don't know what, but I know it was something very serious. Mom never wanted to talk about it, and always told me to forget the past. I have no memories of that August. I've lost a whole month of my life. I tried to get answers from mom, but she would get very upset, and walk away." I began to drift off into memories of trying to get mom to talk, but Tristian nudged me back to the present.

"So anyway" I continued. "I went about daily life, safe in my little bubble. Every morning I got up at six, got ready for school. Jumped on a bus and went to school. Very rarely was I asked to be someone's lab partner, or gym partner. When we had to pair up in any class, it was usually the teachers who paired me with some poor unwilling partner. I kept to myself that entire freshman year. I don't think I spoke more than a handful of words, besides answering a question in class or something like that. I even went out of my way to get my schedule changed so that we would never cross paths. I didn't want you to be the subject of ridicule over tying to protect me. But if we did happen to cross paths, I always waved quickly, and stepped back into my bubble.

"So that's why you stopped speaking to me? All this time I thought I had offended you somehow. I figured you wanted to left alone, so I did. Aww Kikyo, why didn't you ever say anything? I never figured freshman year was so horrible for you. I'm so sorry." He was shaking his head and feeling guilty over my pushing him away. How sad. "No Tristian, don't apologize to me, it's me who should apologize to you. I'm so sorry that I am this pathetic freak that you feel responsible for. Please don't feel that way. This is just who I am". He patted my hand again, urging me to go on once more. "That summer before freshman year, like I said something happened to me, only I can't remember. Sometimes in my dreams I can almost remember, but the memories are incoherent, and fleeting, like dissipating clouds." His expression was so compassionate, that it tore my heart a little.

I needed to continue my story so that he could fully understand. "I can remember the time before anything happening, but then when that particular event happened, it's a blank. I still remember eighth grade, it was the best time for me. We were just kids though. But back to "the event", it was a typical Saturday morning. Mom was getting ready for work, and as I sat at the table drinking some coffee, she was going through my list of chores for the day. I wasn't working yet so her list was the usual. My chores consisted of laundry, dusting, pulling weeds, mowing the lawn, and could I please get around to spider web removal in the basement? I agreed to do as much of her list as was possible, mom knew I was terrified of the basement. She hugged me quickly and kissed the top of my head, and was off to a double shift. I got up washed the 2 coffee cups, and began my chores. As much as I hated that damn basement, I had to at least do the laundry I knew I'd have to do a few loads. I set about to strip the beds, get the clothes in the hamper and fling it all down the stairs. As I set the machine, I came back upstairs and started my dusting. After my dusting and laundry were done, I headed out to the back yard to do some weed pulling. I noticed that the house next door was unusually quiet; they always had people coming and going at all hours of the day or night. I felt uncomfortable, so I rushed to finish my weed pulling, and got to mowing the lawn. I kept feeling that I was being watched. I couldn't shake the thought. I'd feel better once I was back inside." I was pensive for a minute recalling the rest of that fateful day.

"All done with the yard, I headed back in the house. I threw a frozen pack of chicken in the sink and let the water run over it to thaw. I grabbed my school bag and started some homework. I didn't really have much of a life so I was actually ahead of the class in my work. I was about two lessons ahead actually in all my classes. I did some math until I got bored, and decided to do the inevitable, I had been putting off cleaning the basement all day, but it had to be done." I looked into Tristian's eyes then and saw that he was generally interested in what I had to say.

All this time I had been talking he never once stopped to ask a question or interrupt me. He lifted the hand that he had never released, lifted it to his lips, and kissed the back of my hand. He lowered our hands and laced his fingers with mine. I resisted an urge to pull back. This felt good. I smiled weakly at him, and he nodded again for me to continue. "So anyway, I took a deep breath and centered myself, preparing to go in the basement. I ran down the stairs and quickly turned on every light I could find. Unfortunately it wasn't enough. The one bare bulb that hung in the center was dim, as were the two others that were just as dim, and poorly spaced. The only place with bright light was the laundry room, so I left that door open to take full advantage of the light cast from that direction. I got to work. I was a little uneasy, but I always felt like that when I had to go down there. I *think* I saw something move in a far corner and whisper my name, and with my heart thumping in my chest, I inched closer to see what it was . . . . but that's all I remember. Next thing I knew I was in the hospital room with the lights so bright, and my hands and arms bandaged. I was so confused. I was so scared. Mom was there and she had a haggard look in her eyes. She looked so old and tired. I tried to talk but I couldn't find my voice. I had a tube stuck down my throat.

She was stroking my hair, and was kissing my forehead simultaneously. I felt an uncomfortable pinching in my left arm, and saw that I had an I.V. in my arm. My entire body was throbbing with a dulled pain. Why was I here? What had happened? How long was I here? I pleaded with mom to tell me something, anything, but she was crying uncontrollably, and *I had to sooth her.* I was released two days later, after being in the hospital for a week. I was heavily medicated. My head was in such a fog. I couldn't think straight.

When I was finally weaned from the medication, I started asking all those questions that were burning in me. But I knew that mom was so uncomfortable to talk about it. She kept saying that I was safe now. That it was ok. She didn't want me to think about it, so she refused to tell me what had happened. It must've been real bad for her to keep something from me but why? It didn't . . . still doesn't make any sense. Well either way ever since then I was just I guess still in shock. I was uneasy around people. Especially boys and when school started, well I went inside of my safe bubble. But every night it was always the same. During the day I was guarded, and somewhat safe. But at night, I would dream, and try to remember. Fleeting shadows, grasping at thin air, and intense pain and my name being called in a whispering voice is all I could be sure of. All I know was that, whatever happened, it took place in my basement. All mom would tell me for sure was that when she came home, she found me in the dark corner, blood everywhere, my cloths torn, my eyes wild and my body "broken". She said I was shaking uncontrollably, like I was having a seizure or something." "What did she mean by broken?" this was the first time he had spoken up since I had started to tell him my story.

"I honestly don't know what "broken" meant. But I was so soar all over for a very long time. I had bruises that covered my entire body. That's when those memories started to weave into my sub-conscience and my very core was affected. I knew I was a mess, but I had to get on with my life. Everyone thought I was weird anyway, may as well give in to the popular consensus and be weird. I avoided everything and anything as much as possible. Mom had her two jobs, I had school and homework, so when I wasn't at school, I stayed home. It's not like anyone was beating down my door, or the phone was ringing off the hook. But you know I was ok with it. I got used to the loneliness, and moved on. I kept dreaming every night, but that also became routine. I did go out with a group back in sophomore year, we went to a movie, and the whole experience was just awful. After that kids at school talked to me even less than before. I got over it." Tristian could read the hurt and sadness in my eyes, and felt bad for me. "Don't feel bad, Tristian" I said "honestly this is just the way life is for me. I cope and it's all ok really.

"I'd been doing ok I guess since then, until mom got sick anyway. She had said that she had felt a bump on her left breast, and was going to go see the doctor. A few days later the doctor called and told me the news. I was left speechless. Mom was working but I left her a note to wake me when she got home, so that we could talk. I was shocked. What was I going to do? The doctor gave me the number of a lawyer so that mom could put things in order before she was gone. We talked for a very long time that night. I knew she understood that the doctor was right; she didn't even want a second opinion. Anyway, the lawyer fixed it so that I wouldn't lose the house, or have to go to foster care. After mom's death I was legally declared an adult. So I got to stay here." I was fighting back the tears that were threatening to form in my eyes.

"I'm so sorry for all you've been through Kikyo, I really am." He had the saddest look on his face. But somehow I bet mine was twice as low. "I was numb after she was gone. The first two months, I was the living dead.

I existed, barely. But then the nightmares started about four months ago. They were so vivid, but my Swiss cheese brain can't remember them after I wake up. It's so frustrating! I thought I was going crazy after the nightmares began. Every night now or should I say morning, I wake at exactly 3:00, always with the same *feeling*. I'm always so scared, and I startle easily. I could swear I'm seeing shadows move in dark corners, but they don't and footsteps right behind me, but there are none. I'm constantly opening the scratches that are trying to heal all over my body, especially my arms and my neck." He looked at me quizzically, and I realized he hadn't noticed the scratches; I pushed the sleeves of my sweater up to my elbows so that he could see the roadmap that seemed to permanently cover my arms. I then pulled down on the collar so that he could see my neck. The look on Tristian's face was one of horror. I flinched back from the look on his face. He carefully, traced a finger up and down one of my arms, to feel the raised scars.

Poor Tristian, I had no right to unload all this on him. But once I started talking, it was like the flood gates were blown away, and everything that was bottled up inside of me was released in a rush. Would he think I was crazy, he probably wouldn't want to have anything more to do with me after today, and I can't say I blamed him.

I hadn't even told him about my running yet either. Maybe I'd keep the running to myself. It was starting to get late and I was actually getting hungry now. "Tristan, would you like to stay for dinner?" I asked with hope and pleading in my eyes. "Sure, just let me call my mom and tell her that your ok, and I'm staying here a while longer." I gave him the cordless, and went into the kitchen to make dinner. I hadn't really been cooking anymore since mom was gone. It was usually just some cereal, or a sandwich. Since I worked in a restaurant, what was the point? But I did have the essentials to make dinner, and the company to feed it to. I was feeling good about Tristian's visit, and his concern for me. But how far should I let him into my bubble? I wished mom was here so that I could ask her what to do. But the ghost of her voice was in my head as usual and she told me to let him in. It was about time I let someone into my bubble. A tear escaped me, just as Tristian walked into the kitchen, I thought he would take it the wrong way about the tear, but he just wiped it away, and didn't say a word about it. His touch caught me off-guard; I wasn't used to being touched.

We ate dinner, and he wanted to hear more about my past four years. I told him about when I finally got a job. He was pleased that work was an escape for me, even if it was only temporary. I told him about my empty school days, and I knew it was so boring, so I asked him to tell me about his life instead, mine was too sad and pathetic. We talked way into the night and realized it was after nine, on a school night. Tristian had to get home before his dad did, or suffer the consequences of an abusive alcoholic father. He promised to call me from the car, as he drove home, and pick me up the next morning for school.

3:00 a.m., once again, I woke to the sound of my screams, but this time even though the memory was gone as quickly as I realized I was awake, it felt different. I'm not sure exactly how or why, but it was not like the others. Of this I was certain. Hopefully this meant that change was coming soon, and my sanity would return to me after so long of fighting for it. I got ready for my morning run, and had a sneaking suspicion that I wasn't alone. I walked through the house, but of course found nothing. As I stepped out onto the front porch, I scanned the block, but saw nothing out of the ordinary. My neighbors' house was open for business as usual, and the "normal" chaos was going on.

A boy was being initiated into one of the gangs (or out of it, either way it was the same result), the entire gang beat on the poor kid until they all had a turn. But it was worse if you were a girl being initiated, the whole gang would have their way with the girl, until they all had their turn. I cringed at the thought that this could happen to me someday, if they ever set their sights on me. Luckily for me (for once) not even my neighbors' wanted to have anything to do with me. Someone was being thrown out of the crack house for not having any money and the sound of gunshots was in the air a few blocks away towards Armitage. How strange that *this* did not frighten me. It scared me of course, but I left the frightening to my nightmares. The guard to the crack house eyed me as usual, just like every morning as he stood like a sentinel before the doorway. I crossed myself and took off towards the park, not meeting anyone's' gaze for more than a split second.

When I got to North Ave. though, I froze to a stop, as I saw the face from my nightmares! I recognized him immediately, although I had never met this man. My blood turned to ice, and my brain screamed for me to run! But my feet had turned to lead and I couldn't move them. The face stared at me from at least a block away, nevertheless I *knew* that face. He was still a stranger to me, but I had seen that face before night after night. He didn't move, or react to me in any way. His face was a blank slate, and his eyes were the same black rimmed neon red from my dreams. Was I still dreaming? My mind snapped back to me in an instant, and I whirled around to flee back home. I couldn't understand how this could be. I must still be dreaming. But as I retreated, everything was so real. It didn't feel like a dream.

Never once did I look back, I ran as fast as my feet could carry me, it felt like I was shot from a rocket. I took the 11 steps to my front door in two, and threw myself into my house. I peeked through the blinds, but saw nothing. Should I call the cops? I began to argue with myself then. "Yeah right" I said aloud, "Call the cops and say what? Officer this is an emergency, my nightmares are trying to get me!" sure, they'd put me on the top of the list after that. After a solid 10 minutes of searching the poor view I had of the street, I gave up. I had calmed down enough to pry myself away from the window, and go to take a bath. I was imagining it was all. My dreams have me so worked up that now I'm seeing things in real life. I tried to console myself, but I was doing a poor job.

As I undressed, I saw I still had goose bumps all over my body, and I was covered in a film of cold sweat. I filled the tub with hot water, watching as the steam rose, and as I perched on the edge of the tub, I tried to focus my thoughts on the face I had seen. But who was he? I had never seen him before, and now that I thought about it, he had no expression on his face. I *needed* to know who this man was. Why did I freeze and panic when I saw him? He was just a man on the street, probably just a drunk. I tried to rationalize with myself, but how could I convince myself otherwise, if I knew in my soul that this was the person staring in my nightmares night after horrific night? I slipped into the scalding water and let it melt my too tensed body. I was still shivering from the adrenaline in my system. But I had to laugh to myself as I thought, with all the adrenaline in my system every day, if I were to take a drug test I'd probably fail, and I didn't even do drugs.

After my bath, I got dressed for school, had some breakfast, and headed for the door, to get to the bus stop. I was not paying attention, so when I opened the door to step out, to my amazement, Tristian was at my door about to ring the bell. My usual mask of sadness, and loneliness, mixed with stress, dissolved into one of pure joy. He actually came back. I hadn't scared him away like I thought I had. He kept his promise to pick me up for school today. He walked me to his car, which he had left double parked, to ring the bell, and as he opened the door for me, I felt good again, just like yesterday. Tristian gave me a quick hug before shutting my door. And I smiled to myself, as I erased the memory of my morning run for the moment.

Once he got into the car and shut the door, Tristian turned to me with a big grin; it would've lit his face if not for the hint of sadness in his eyes. "Kikyo, you really didn't expect me to be here today did you?" he asked me matter-of-factly. I nodded my head in agreement, and all I could say was sorry. He drove with one hand while the other never released mine. As rays of hope slowly began to creep into my sub-conscience, I looked at Tristian with a grateful glance, and averted my eyes when he turned to look at me. He lifted my hand to his lips and kissed the back of my hand. He didn't try to converse further, sensing my reluctance. He just held my hand until we arrived at school, and parked the car in his usual spot.

As Tristian cut the engine off, he turned to look at me, and said he hoped I had a good day. We both knew that I had gone out of my way to work my class schedule so that I wouldn't have to run into him, so I knew I wouldn't see him again, until the end of the day. It was going to be a long day, but at least I was able to look forward to seeing him later after school. I also had to go to work today, if I still had a job. Having lost two entire days, put me behind at work, and school, but then again I was ahead in all my classes, so it didn't really affect me. Tristian promised to meet me at my locker at the end of the day, to take me home. I thanked him for everything, for the ride, for attention, but most of all for his friendship. He gave me a quick awkward hug seeing as we were still in the car, which left me feeling slightly stunned (as I wasn't expecting it), and with a wink he got out of the car, to open my door for me. When I got out, he took me in his arms again, "now for a proper hug" he said to me with a big smile across his beautiful face.

After Tristian released me unwillingly, I set out to face the day. I took a deep breath and prepared myself for whatever awaited me today. As I passed people in the halls, on my way to, from, and during classes, I heard the whispers, and I felt the stares all day long. I knew Tristian was popular, he was the star athlete, he was gorgeous and he was wasting time with me. This must've been horrifying for the "in-crowd". But if he chose to be my friend after I had pushed him away so long ago, I wasn't going to stop him. I went about my day as usual; it was like as soon as he was out of sight, my invisible bubble popped up again and in I went, except that this time I was paying attention to what was going on around me. I was listening to what the entire student body of Steinmetz High had to say about Tristian and I. And boy were they creative.

True to his word, Tristian was at my locker at the end of the day. He was casually leaning against it, ignoring everyone around him but still scanning the crowd looking for me. When he saw me, his eyes lit up like a Christmas tree, and a smile played across his lips. When I got to the locker, he opened his arms to embrace me, and I blushed so deep that I was sure I was red as a tomato. It was awkward for me and somewhat embarrassing. People actually stopped to stare. How rude! I went stiffly into his embrace, and he kissed the top of my head. After I exchanged books, Tristian took my hand, and led the way to his car. I was feeling kind of flustered, and worry was creeping up on me. I had to know what his intentions were before I let this go on much longer but not with all the eyes watching and ears listening.

I was still blushing, as he held the door to his vintage 69' Ford Mustang rag-top convertible open for me to get in. when he got in the car, he took my hand again, and I pulled away. He put the car in gear and started towards my house. "Tristian, I think we need to talk." I stammered, and tore my eyes away from his mesmerizing gaze. "What exactly are we doing here? I mean I know it's obvious I like you, I always have, but why on earth are you doing this? I'm a mess, in so many different ways. You're too good for me, and I just don't fit in with people. What will they . . . . what are they already saying about you? I could care less about what they think of me, but you, your type is way beyond me." A stray tear escaped me, and I wiped it away quickly. I knew all I was doing was crushing any chance at happiness I might have with Tristian. But it was better now than later when it would hurt way too much.

He held a finger to my lips to shush me, and with the kindest eyes, he melted my heart. "Kikyo, do you honestly believe that I *care* what the entire student body of Steinmetz High School thinks about me? I only care that you realize and understand that you are worth someone caring about you. You've been through so much, and no one has been by your side. I could kick myself for letting you shut me out. But we were still kids then, and there was nothing I could have done for you. But I guess if I had just known how much pain you were in, at least I could've let you cry on my shoulder." Now what is all this nonsense about? Did someone say something to you? If they did say or do anything to you, they will need to answer to me." Anger started to creep into his face, and I nodded no. No one had said anything *to* me, just about me, about Tristian, and about "us".

"I don't ever want *me* to be the reason you're sad. I can't bear to cause you any additional pain. You have enough of your own already. I know you think you're so strong, but I can look in your big brown eyes and know in my soul, that you're hurting. It's not fair for the stupid empty bobble-headed girls to treat you like they do. I know what they say, and I know what the guy jerks say too. But rest assured Kikyo no one will bother you. And if anyone gets out of line . . . well lets just say, sorry for them. I looked at him quizzically, and he explained.

"It really all started when we began freshman year. Everyone knew that something had happened to you over the summer, but since you couldn't remember, they all came up with their own conclusions. Some said you were into drugs, or you had been "initiated" into your neighborhood gang. Others thought you were into "cutting" yourself. And especially, since your arms were always bandaged or covered up, I guess I kind of believed it too. I thought you had snapped from that unknown event, and started cutting in order to cope." My mind was racing. "I knew the kids all talked about me" I said, "but never like this. All those idiots cared about was that I was a source of gossip and giggles for them. I'm glad I at least amused them all. To think, they actually thought I would deliberately cut myself because I had been gang raped in order to join a stupid gang? How sadistic do they think I am? It's been four years, and you thought that way too?" I could hardly believe what I was hearing! If it weren't for the fact that the car was in motion, I would have jumped out. I was fuming by the time we got to my house. It was a short 20 minute ride, but nonetheless it felt like an eternity to me.

"Kikyo, please let me explain" he pleaded "how was I supposed to know what was going on? You refused to speak to me. Your mom would tell mine that she couldn't get you to talk to her either. In this neighborhood anything could happen. How can you blame me for thinking the worse, if you yourself don't even know what happened to you?" Tristian looked like I felt, we were both so wound up over this that we both needed to calm down. When we got to my block, I had to make this right between us, I had him pull the car into the garage beside my wagon, so that it wouldn't have to sit out in the street and God forbid something happen to it. We rode the rest of the way in silence, but he never let go of my hand. And truthfully, I didn't want him to.

We entered the house from the back yard, and into the kitchen, so that I could call off work. I explained to my boss, that I was going through a difficult time in my life right now and could I please have a few weeks off? He was very understanding, and told me to call him when I was ready to come back. I actually only had this job as a favor to my mom, so the favor continued long after she was gone. I didn't want to think of what I was going to do in the meantime, but I needed some time off. And my boss was very understanding.

After I hung up the phone, I smiled sadly at Tristian in apology, but his look mirrored mine. We had nothing to forgive each other for. As he leaned against my kitchen door, he opened his arms wide for me, and I let him envelope me in them. He held me close, and I felt that sense of safety, and protection from him. I snuggled into his ripped muscular chest, and inhaled his scent. I knew he would never intentionally hurt me. So many years of hurt, pain, confusion and depression, all began to slip away, as he held me tight, and whispered in my hair, that he would keep me safe. I could go on like this forever, but I knew in my core that this happiness was only temporary; my horror would creep up on me again, as soon as I fell into my nightmarish sleep tonight. Tristan could possibly do all he can to physically protect me, but I was on my own when it came to protecting me from myself. He kissed my head, and took my hands in his to kiss them too. I wanted to cry from the sweet sentiment, but I kept the tears at bay.

Tristian stayed for dinner after calling his mom to let her know where he was. We talked about him mostly, his school activities, his friends, his mom, but we never broached the subject about his dad. I knew this was a sensitive issue because his dad was an alcoholic that took his benders out on Tristian and his mom, but mostly on Tristian. My poor Tristian, he had enough to deal with without me adding my tremendous burden to him as well. We talked until it got dark outside, and I just couldn't bear that he had to drive through my neighborhood at night. But I knew he had to go. It wasn't proper for him to stay in my house overnight. We said our unwilling goodbyes, and he promised to pick me up for school tomorrow, and to be on the cell with me the whole ride home.

As soon as Tristian pulled out of my garage, I ran inside the house to grab the phone. I felt like I talked non-stop, who knew I had so much to say? We talked about our grade school times (those were much happier times for both of us). We talked about what the future held for us after graduation, Tristan was going, to my surprise to Triton Community College, out in River Grove only a few blocks from where the Movie Theater was. To my surprise because this is where I decided I was going. I felt like my planets were finally aligning, and my life was headed for happiness. But could it last? Could I make it out of high school in one piece? I knew that with Tristian by my side, it was all going to be all right. The real question was could I hold it together until graduation? My answer to this was; I had better.

The winds of change were blowing, but I still had that irking feeling that as positive as I was about my new life situation, some of the prior gloom was bound to sneak back in. Tristan got to his house and it was time to hang up. We said our good nights and he promised to be at my house in the morning for school. Tristian had mentioned earlier today that he had a meet after school, and he wanted me there, I knew it would be awkward and uncomfortable for me, but if he wanted me there I would suck it up and go. I threw my I-pod and a book into my bag, just in case I couldn't cope with the meet, I'd go and wait by Tristian's car. I promised myself that I would make an attempt to leave myself open to conversation with my classmates, while I was in the bleachers, as Tristian competed. And as I got ready for bed, I had a stern conversation with myself that no matter what I dreamt of, I would NOT go running, even if it meant I was doing housework or making dinner at three in the morning.

I was running again on my usual path, but this time when I saw those eyes at the end of the block, I didn't freeze. This time I was running to them! I couldn't stop myself, it's like I was being pulled by some unknown magnetic force. But the faster I ran towards that face, the farther away it also got. I was running as if on a treadmill. I know my feet were moving, but I couldn't really feel the pavement under them. Those eyes, those eyes bore into mine, beckoning me closer, challenging me closer, and daring me to come closer. I couldn't see the features of the face, just those eyes. From where I stood, me at one end of the block, he at the other, those eyes were hard and black with a ring of what looked like neon red. Was that possible? Who was he? Those eyes were mesmerizing and enchanting me. I heard a dog barking in the distance and he looked away for the tiniest fraction of a second. This broke the magnetic pull, and I spun on my heels to run. I ran back home again, back to my safety. I ran back to my empty lonely house, full of shadows, and foggy memories. Once again I flew up the stairs, and into my house, only to find that those eyes were there waiting for me in my house! He was standing in the hallway, as I flung the door open! As if in slow motion, I fell backwards down the front porch steps as I screamed!

I was screaming myself awake again, but this time, I knew why I was so scared. I usually forgot what my dreams were as soon as I opened my eyes, but today was different. I was shaking all over, in a cold sweat. The tears were running down my eyes, and I was sobbing so hard my lungs hurt.

Those eyes were all I could think of. They held no emotion; they just shone their neon red, and bore into my soul, like they were reading every thought and memory I had ever had. Once I got a hold of myself, I got up for my morning shower. The hot water stung my new scratches and I was still shaking, when the water had run cold. But I had to put it out of my mind, for the sake of my sanity, and also because I didn't want to concern Tristian about this. I could handle it; I had done so alone for so long now. No, I would not tell him about this.

I was determined to make this a good day. Tristian was running today after school, and it was only fair that I be there to support him. So I got dressed and ready for school. I pushed the clouds away from my mind, and concentrated on being positive. I was nibbling on my right thumb nail deep in concentration, a nervous habit of mine while I was waiting for him out on the front porch. I didn't want him to Double Park long while he waited for me. My heart skipped a beat when he beeped the horn and broke me out of my concentration. When he was in front of my house, he jumped out of the car to get my door. He gave me a lingering hug, and held me slightly closer than he ever had. He must've seen the deep lost in thought look on my face.

Once in the car, he put it in gear, and took my hand, intertwining his fingers with mine. This felt good and safe. It was warm, despite the fact that it was only late April. I wore a light sweater, just to cover my arms. I didn't want Tristian to discover my new bleeding scratches. We drove in silence, he was very cautious around me, like I was made of glass and he was afraid to break me. He didn't want to say nor do anything that would make me shut him out again. And I actually silently thanked him for the quiet, with a squeeze to his hand. I continued to chew on my thumbnail, all the way to school. Never once did he ask me what was on my mind.

As he pulled into the lot at school, people turned to stare as they saw me in his car. The gossip started again even before we were out of the car. "Kikyo, don't let it get to you, they're just jealous, that I got the hottest girl in school." He finally said breaking out silence. "Yeah, like I'm falling for that line" I said in a grumble. "Anyway, I think you have it backwards, I have the hottest guy in school. Look at you, your perfect. You're like a foot taller than my 5'2", you have the perfect features, perfect hair, and . . ." I went on with a serious blush, "you have the perfect body. No wonder, they all think you've lost your mind. How can I fairly compete? I'm short and average. I don't stand out at all, which is actually a good thing, because I couldn't deal with attention if I was pretty, *and* a freak. How could I possibly be in the same league as the likes of say someone like Elizabeth Conner?" the words spilled out of me faster than I could stop them. The ominous clouds in my brain started to creep in on me then.

Elizabeth Connor was of course the cheerleader captain, and the "Goddess" of Steinmetz High. Long blond hair, aqua blue eyes, perfect skin, and enough money to buy all her friendships and loyal followers that worship the pedicured ground she walked on. I knew Tristian and Elizabeth had dated from sophomore and junior years. "Kikyo, don't you ever, ever compare yourself to that superficial empty-headed moron. You are far superior, and her artificial looks will fade away after a few years, but your beauty is timeless. Your inner beauty, goes deep and shines through, hers is just surface level. Elizabeth Connor is not who I want. I want only you. And her dislike for you is like I said jealousy. She wishes, I'd give her the time of day, but my time is all yours. So do with me what you will, and ignore that inconsequential wench. I'm all yours for as long as you'll have me. But we gotta go or we'll be late. We can talk about this later. See you on the field after school?" he smiled down at me, and I nodded. "Good, let's go." He opened my door for me and hugged me tight for a second, as he kissed the top of my head. I squeezed him just a little tighter, and kissed his chest. Then we were off to face the wild jungle that was our high school once again.

Chapter Three

Tristian

I retreated to my safe bubble as soon as we were off in different directions to our classes. The rumor mill was in overdrive all day, and I was a little uncomfortable about going to see him run, but I had promised myself that I would do it for Tristian. I would be there for him, just like he's been here for me. I knew it would be hard, but I vowed to *not* sit in a corner. I was going to against my years of solitude, and be front and center. And if the entire student body of C.P. Steinmtez couldn't deal with it, then they would just have to leave.

I had made a stern vow to myself, but I wondered just how hard it would be to keep my promise. But I was determined, and it was about time that I didn't fade into a dark corner, this was about Tristian, not me. So when he jogged onto the field, to get ready for his race, I was on my feet in an instant, with the crowd, and as he scanned the sea of faces, his eyes found mine, and the wide grin that dimpled his cheeks I so loved, sent my heart into a flurry of flip flops. He winked at me and then he was off.

He ran like the wind. Tristian left his opponents in the dust, and the crowd went wild, I along with them. I actually was having conversations with the people around me. They were curious about Tristian and I, and since I was so overjoyed watching Tristian win over and over I let my guard down, and had a good time. I had not felt so much joy since back in grade school when we were both just kids, and nothing complicated our childhoods. At the end of all the races, he took his rightful place, to receive his first place medal, and I was so proud for him, I could burst. My face actually hurt from all the smiling I had done while I watched him run. But for once, it was a good hurt. This hurt, I could live with.

As the crowd continued to cheer, some girls actually congratulated me on being with Tristian, and me finally looking happy for a change. Tristian jumped into the bleachers, as hands clapped him on the back and gave him high fives, and tried to grab at him, he ignored them, and came straight for me. He picked me up in an awkward embrace, and kissed my forehead. "Kikyo, aw I can't tell you how happy I am that you decided to stay. Did you have a good time?" He was beaming, and so was I, the crowd began to dissipate, and he took me by the hand, to lead me to the field. I was so happy for him. It was actually a very good day.

Even though he was all sweaty, I still hugged him tight to me every chance I got as we worked our way out of the bleachers. We tuned everyone out and it was just us. Tristian's coach was calling up to him, to "Shower-Up". He smiled down at me, and led me back to the locker rooms, where I sat in the hall waiting for him to be done. The hall was empty as I was leaning against the cold wall. I had pushed up the sleeves of my sweater, and was absentmindedly, tracing, the scars over my arms. It felt like my skin was embossed, with a confusing and terrifying roadmap. My arms didn't hurt anymore, and the bleeding had eventually stopped, but I knew I would inevitably re-open my many wounds. I tried to push the thought out of my mind, and concentrate on my good day. It was my first good day in my almost four years at Steinmetz High. The girls that were in the bleachers to me were very nice, and I think I even had a class with one of them. For once I didn't need to hide in a corner, and shut out what people said about me. The girls were actually; glad to see me animated, and happy, in contrast to my usual dark gloomy self.

I heard Tristian talking to one of his teammates, as he was being congratulated on his win, so I quickly pulled my sleeves back down, and stood up. As he emerged, he flashed a grin my way, and held his arms open for me to come to him. We fit together perfectly, like two pieces of a puzzle. He gave me a gentle squeeze, and kissed the top of my head, before he took my hand and kissed it, then led me out of the school, and to the car. "Thank you for being here today, I really appreciate that you stayed, it means a lot to me. *You* mean a lot to me. I hope you really had a good time, because it sure looked like it. Kikyo honey, you were radiant!" The way his eyes bore into my soul, was like he had x-ray vision, and could read all my secrets. I shifted in his embrace, slightly uncomfortable, but I still managed to kiss his chest, and pull him just a little closer.

Once we were in the car, I asked him if he would stay with me for a while, or if he had to get home. I knew how his dad got if he'd been drinking, he was like a live grenade that had lost its' pin. I wanted Tristian with me, but I didn't want to cause him any trouble. "Oh Kikyo, honey, of course I'll stay with you. Like I told you before, you're who matters to me most. And anyway I can't bear to leave you all alone in that house, and especially in that neighborhood. It tears me apart to know that anything can happen to you, and I'm nowhere to save you. Kikyo, this may come as a shock to you, but even through all those years of keeping me at bay, I never forgot you, I always kept an eye out for you. I knew how much you wanted to be left alone, but how could I honestly, walk away? Darling, you're my other half, you're the air I breathe, and the sun that warms me, even though for the past four years, you've been a perpetual eclipse, still it didn't matter, if you couldn't be my sun, I guess then I'd settle for the moon." Was this real, was he just proclaiming his true feelings to me? I knew he like me, I wasn't an idiot but this was deep. I thought I was the only one who felt like this. What a fool I'd been, wasting so many years, over what exactly I still didn't know. But I couldn't tell him I felt the same. I wouldn't tell him. I didn't want to eventually hurt him. I would vow to myself, to not have to put him through any kind of hurt or pain.

When we got to my house, I told him to park in the garage, and as I got out to manually open the door, I thought I saw someone for a split second, but whatever it was, if anything had ever really been there, it was gone as soon as I acknowledged it. I shook it off, and let it go. There was plenty of time for paranoid delusions, once Tristian left. Right now belong to Tristian and me. As soon as we were in my kitchen, he shut the door behind him, and pulled me close to him, I let my bag fall to floor, and I hugged him tight. I snuggled my face into his muscular chest, and he kissed the top of my head, and then my forehead, but I froze as I realized the direction he was going in. when he felt me stiffen, without a word, he squeezed me gently, and kissed my head again and released me. He knew I wasn't ready for this, and I silently thanked him for not pushing it. This boy was a saint; he was so perfect in so many ways, so why was he wasting his time with the likes of me? I couldn't understand what he possibly saw in me. But he obviously wanted me, and I wanted him, so I would try to let it go and enjoy him for as long as I could.

"Tristian" I asked, when we were sitting on the couch, not really watching the television, "what do you possibly see in me that keeps you around me? I've shut you out, I've been rude, and I've been an empty shell for so long, what can I possibly offer you? I have nothing to give. Whatever it is that happened to me so long ago drained everything that I had in me. I was happy once, a long time ago but all that has since past. I truly want to be happy again but I fear that I'm just going to end up hurting you and this time it will be harder because I'd know I was doing it and I won't be able to stop myself. If we let this . . . "us" go on, no good can come of it. It may be fun for a while but not in the long run." My tears of despair slowly ran out of my eyes unconsciously, and I could feel my heart begin to fissure. I swore to myself I wouldn't go this route, but I couldn't help myself.

"Kikyo, how are you gonna tell me, what's good for me? *You're* what's good for me, do you honestly think, I just bared my soul for anything other than love? You think its fun for me to have seen you in so much pain that all you could do to cope was turn into the living dead? I'm not like all those idiots at school, I knew you before your incident, and I'd love nothing better than to get you there again. Honey you can't do it alone, let me help you. Let me chase away all those dark clouds that cover your heart, let me help you shine again. Whatever happened to you was a tragedy, but it's time you move on, and let someone take care of you for a change. Won't you let me be your safety net? Trust in me, when I say that I'm here for as long as you want me and need me, I am yours to do with what you will, but I refuse to walk away again like I did before. You're too important to me, to see you fade away again like you did the past four years." His eyes were so consumed with emotion that he had to turn away from me, so that I wouldn't see that his eyes were tearing up as well. I hadn't officially declared anything to him, and already I was hurting him.

"Tristian, like I said I don't want to be the cause of any pain for you, but if this is how you feel, I may as well tell you how I feel." He took my hand in his and steadied himself for what I was about to say, not knowing which direction I was leaning towards. "Look, I told you before, that I was a mess. I've been so dazed and confused for the past four years, and I don't know why. I've kept everyone at bay and I don't know why. I've been in my little protective bubble for so long now, that for me to get out, or let someone in, honestly frightens me. I've had years of physiological abuse from my own nightmares, that it's a wonder I can function at all. If it weren't for the fact that I had mom, I would've killed myself long ago. After I sent you packing, all I had to live for was my mom, but now she's gone. What ties do I have to this impossible life now? Trust me dear, your better off without me, but on the other hand, I can't ignore the way I feel about you. Thanks to you, I learned to try to smile again, I'm happy when I'm with you, it kills me when you go home, and I'm left here all alone to face my own personal demons. I'm torn between myself, do I let you go now, before it's too late, and continue in my misery? Or do I dare let myself be happy, even if it is briefly?"

I knew that mom never knew I had suicidal tendencies, I don't think even I knew it until I voiced it out loud, but I was tired, my brain was choking on the fog that consumed it, and my heart ached for the lack of love it craved. So I questioned myself again, "Do I dare be happy?" could I even possibly leave my bubble, and once again be normal? I didn't have the answer to those questions yet, but I was willing to find them. Tristian smiled at me, that smile that sent chills up and down my spine and said, "Kikyo, honey . . . please, please, I beg you . . . . dare to be happy"

"Tristian" I began with a deep sigh, "I *want* to be happy, and I want *you* to be the one who makes it so." My tears overflowed, as I saw the flicker of joy in his eyes. "I promise I will never intentionally hurt you, I promise that I will never shut you out again, and I promise to attempt to pop that bubble once and for all. I promise to dare to be happy. I love you Tristian, and I was incomplete for so long, that I felt I was missing a part of me, and now I know that part I was missing was you. I wonder if when I'm finally happy enough to sleep through an entire night, the nightmares will continue to torment me. I hope not. I've got you to live for now, and I don't plan on giving you up any time soon. So I hope you can cope with the neurotic mess that is me." We were both grinning by this time, and bursting at the seams. "You do realize that you picked one messed-up crazy chic, to fall for right?" I teased. And his response sent butterflies scattering in my stomach, "Yes, but you're *my* messed-up crazy chic." We embraced for a long lingering moment after that, and he slowly and carefully, bent to kiss me, but when I shifted, he kissed my head instead.

It was time for Tristian to leave, and it took all my strength to not hold him tight and ask him to stay. Even though we declared ourselves openly, it still wasn't proper to have him stay in my house overnight. So I had to fight hard with myself to let him go. "Tristian, amor, can you do me a favor? Are you doing anything tomorrow?" I asked. "Querida, whatever you need just ask me, I am all yours remember?" I nodded. "Amor, look I think it's time I cleaned out mom's room, but I cant bear to go in there alone, maybe with you at my side, I can face her room, and it will help in my healing process." "Kikyo darling, I'll be here bright and early, don't you worry about a thing querida, I'm here for you. Now I do really have to go. But I would love nothing better than to stay with you, and protect you through the night." I nodded in agreement, and kissed his chest, as he held me close.

Tristian called me as soon as he was out of the garage, and we talked about the race today. Again I congratulated him on his win, and told him how grateful I was for him. We said our goodnights' and hung up. I was floating on cloud nine by the time I crawled into bed. I was determined to turn my life around and finally be done with my depression, and let my guard down for once in four years. It was about time that I took control of my life instead of letting it control me.

I was in bed not really asleep and dreaming yet, just letting my mind wander. I was thinking about Tristian. I had never thought too much about him physically, until now. I imagined what it would be like to trace my hands over his body. To feel all his muscles, and learn every dimple and crease on him. I imagined running my fingers through his chocolate brown, shoulder length hair, as I untied the band he used to keep it in a ponytail. I imagined kissing his bare chest, and nuzzling his neck. But most of all I reveled in what it would be like to finally kiss him, and feel his lips on mine.

With these happy images I drifted to sleep, with Tristian's name on my lips, I fell away to unconsciousness.

I was running yet again, with a sense of urgency that, I felt was a little unusual. I was running on the normal path, around Humboldt Park, and felt not just one pair of eyes on me but many. I could feel my heart thumping wildly in my chest trying to break free from the confines of my chest. I could feel the ground beneath my feet, trying to hold me in place and forbid me to run. I could smell an acrid scent in the air, kind of like singed hair. I could actually taste the heaviness of the scent that was burning my throat. Panic seized me and I stood frozen in place yet again, as those neon eyes stared at me from a block away. But I was ready to face him this time, to see what compelled me to stay and not flee. I was determined to break this unnerving cycle, and take my life back. But the odd thing about this nightmare was that it really didn't feel like a dream. I think I was conscience, I felt like I was conscience, but was I really? Those blood red neon eyes never left mine for a moment, and as I walked slowly and steadily towards them, it was like I was being pulled by an invisible force. I walked at a slow pace, and inched my way closer to him. His gaze beckoned me to come, and I did.

Shadows moved in my peripheral vision, but I didn't turn to them, my eyes were locked on his eyes. I could feel the electricity, emanating from him, and kept my steady pace towards him. The air now smelled metallic, and heavy. For some reason I wasn't afraid for once. I was curious, but cautious, was I finally going to get some answers? I felt the shadows moving with me, they followed close, but just out of my sight, I could hear fabric rustling as they moved, and it reminded me of dry leaves in the fall.

I was half-way up the block, and he stood unwavering for me to come closer. I steeled myself, and put my emotions in check. He was holding a hand out to me, as I closed the distance between us. It was so dark out, that I wondered why the streetlights were out. The only light came from the moon, no not the moon, it was a cloudy night, and the light source came from him. His face and hands radiated the light. I was drawn to his light like a moth to a flame. I was about an arms length from him, when a dog barked in the distance, and broke my concentration. I looked away for a split second, and when I turned back to see him, it was Tristian I finally saw behind the blood-red neon eyes! He had a snarl on his lips, and looked at me like he would devour me in an instant.

The rustling of the shadows, got louder and the dog in the distance howled a warning to me. I was frozen with terror, as my nightmare Tristian, grabbed me, in an instant, and plunged his teeth into my throat! I tried to fight, but it was pointless, I may have as well been fighting smoke. I tried to scream in agony and horror but no sound came from me, as he continued to drain me. And the rustling shadows began to bite me all over and drink! I felt weightless and numb; I was slipping into total darkness. I was floating into oblivion. And I heard that dog barking again urgently louder this time, like it was coming closer.

I was clawing at my neck when I awoke; I was disoriented and sobbing hard. I was shaking so ferociously that it felt like an earthquake on my bed. What had I dreamed of? Now I couldn't remember. I knew I was bleeding again, before I even untangled myself from the sheets. My hands trembled terribly as I reached out to my nightstand to get a sip of water from the glass I placed there every night. The water sloshed around and out of the glass spilling all over the place, as I dropped the glass. It shattered into a million pieces, and water was everywhere. I couldn't control my sobbing, and my lungs ached from the force of every heaving breath.

I rose from my bed, unsteadily, wobbling slightly. Once I was sure of my footing, I went to inevitably wash up, shower, and doctor my wounds.

What I saw in the mirror shocked me. My eyes had changed from their normal milk chocolate brown to gold, I was guessing from the emotion. My eyes used to change color with my emotions, or should I say when I used to have emotions. But this was entirely new. Never had I had such a strong reaction as to change them to gold. This morning my neck took the blunt of the damage, as I clawed my way out of my nightmare. I was bleeding slightly more than usual considering, my wounds were deeper today. I cleaned them with antiseptic, and stepped into the hot water in the tub to release my tension. I knew that Tristian would be worried about the new scratches, but it was something I had no control over. I ran a finger over the deepest gouge on my neck and was surprised it was so hot and deep.

My body was itchy somehow, as if my foot had fallen asleep, only it wasn't just my foot. The itch was inside of me, and I couldn't scratch deep enough to ease it. I slumped down in the hot water until I was completely covered by it. It felt good to be warm and safe. I stayed under, even when the air in my lungs began to run out. Behind my eyes I saw the red neon eyes of the Tristian-man in my dreams at the end of the block. I tried to will myself out from under the water but, it was like he kept me under water with just a glance, and then with my last seconds of air in me, I shut my eyes against the water, and slid into unconsciousness yet again.

"Kikyo, Kikyo honey, can you hear me? Please come back to me, please!" I could hear Tristian calling to me, but he was so far away I could barely hear him. And then I felt and uncomfortable pressure on my chest every few seconds, it came and went. My lungs burned, and I was so cold. "Kikyo, Kikyo, stay with me honey!" Why was Tristian screaming? He was screaming but was so far away. Was I dreaming again? The pain in my lungs was getting stronger, and my chest was too heavy. I felt Tristan's lips on mine and his hot breath breathing life into me. This snapped me from my confusion and I shot up like a bullet. What on earth was going on? Suddenly I heard Tristian not two inches from my face, screaming at me to come back, and was he crying? I opened my eyes, and as I tried to focus, he relaxed and held me tight to his chest. The combination of coughs and sobs that erupted from me sent blazing chills to my core. What had happened to me? I was cold and wet, and then I realized that all I had on was towel! The horror! What the hell happened? "Tristian, what happened?" I was hysterical by this time, and he was getting himself under control. "Tristian why am I naked? What the hell is going on?" "Oh God, Kikyo, I thought I was gonna lose you! Why did you try to drown yourself?" His eyes were pleading with me for an answer to which I had none. "Darling" he said, now trying control of himself "get dressed and we'll talk. I'll make you some tea."

Tristian, left the bathroom to give me a chance to dry off and get dressed, I was in a state of pure confusion. After I dressed, I took a look at myself in the mirror, and saw my morning scratches, once again. I looked frightening, but what could I do? After pulling my hair up in a ponytail, I came out to the kitchen where he was already sipping on some tea, and a steaming cup waited for me. He looked at me with worry on his face;

I guess he was still trying to control himself when he took a look at my neck, because he had to look away. I was wearing a long sleeved tee shirt, and my neck was exposed.

"Tristian, what happened?" I pleaded with him for an answer all the while trying to keep my emotions in check. "Kikyo, honey are you all right? Did someone try to hurt you?" he was still on the verge of hysteria, but was able to keep it at bay. "Kikyo, baby I was so scared when I called you this morning, and you didn't answer. I came over immediately! When you wouldn't open the door, I did all I could think of. Sorry honey but I owe you a new kitchen door." I turned to follow his gaze at what was left of my door. It hung by only the top hinge, and the frame was terribly splintered. "Kikyo, what happened?" He asked again, as he opened his arms for me to come to him. "I don't know for sure" I stammered out so low I don't really think he heard me. "I . . . I . . ." I trailed off as the sobs finally consumed me, and I cried into his chest and ruined his shirt. He held me tighter than ever before, and let me cry until my sobs slowly faded away. When I had composed myself enough to unbury my face from his chest, he led me to the living room, so that we could talk better. As we settled onto the couch, he pulled me closer and took my hands in his. It seemed to me that this was a pose we would repeat time after time.

"After you left last night, I dreamed about you, and it was nice." I blushed at the memory of my pre-dream. "It's a little embarrassing, but all I'll say was that it wasn't bad, pleasant actually. But after that, I don't really remember much except that I was running, and I could smell something like maybe lightning, but of course I'm not sure about that. And then there were the eyes . . ." I trailed off as I remembered the red neon eyes yet again, and began to tremble but whose were they? "Then when I screamed myself awake, I went to take a bath, and I guess I fell asleep. The water was so comfortable and warm, how long was I under?" I actually wondered what time it was now, just to do the mental math myself.

"Amor, its 7:30-ish now, I don't know how long you were under, but let me tell you my version of this ok?" Tristian took a deep breath, and continued. "I was so excited about being with you all day today that I could hardly sleep. I dreamed of you as well amor. But when I got up at five this morning, I called you to see if you were up, I knew it was early, but you've told me you get up early, why I still don't understand. Anyway, when you didn't answer, I got worried. I didn't want to even think what had gone on. I jumped in my car and was here in ten minutes. By the way,

I broke the lock on the garage door too. Sorry. So I banged on the back door, and when you didn't answer, I came around the front, but you didn't get that door either. I was half out of my mind by this time, and your neighbors were watching me intensely. I came back to the back door and pounded again, but when you still didn't open, I broke it down. I could see the faint light from under the bathroom, and I knocked first, but still no answer from you. God Kikyo, I was so scared. I let myself in and found you floating in the water. I went mad to see you like that! I thought I was too late and I had lost you. I pulled you out and started CPR. I checked your pulse to see if you still had one Thank God! Your pulse was weak, but I worked on you for a few minutes, until you came back to me." His voice broke off with a choke, and I looked up from my lap, to see the fear in his eyes. "Kikyo, why would you try to kill yourself? What are you running from? Please talk to me I want to understand what is going on with you. Please don't shut me out again. I don't think I can go through it this time, you mean so much more to me now.

"Querido, even I don't know what's going on, I keep having these nightmares and they must be so real, because I'm hurting myself while I'm asleep, and I don't know why!" I started to sob, I was getting hysterical again as I ran my hand across my neck. "I think I need therapy or something, maybe hypnosis, I don't know. I need something. But the thing is, after I'm awake, I'm ok. I don't understand it. But maybe if . . . if . . ." I trailed off, trying to say the words before I knew what I was going to say. "Maybe if" Tristian jumped in "Maybe if I stayed tonight, just to wake you before you hurt yourself." He looked at me with anxious eyes, then stammering he continued "Kikyo, it would be strictly for your safety, I'm not trying to give you the wrong impression." I was blushing at the forgotten memory that he had pulled me out of the tub naked. And I wasn't as embarrassed about the fact that I was nude, but the fact that he saw all my scars. Tristian quickly saw my blush, and figured I was embarrassed about the nudity, and tried to ease the tension. "Kikyo, look as soon as I saw you under the water, my mind went into overdrive, and trust me I saw nothing. I pulled you out of the water, and covered you with a towel. Please don't be embarrassed about that. Trust me amor, I respect you way too much, to take advantage of you hon. just think about it, and I'll do whatever you want me to do." He pulled me to him, and hugged me tight, kissing my forehead. Oh how difficult it would be if he were to ever leave me, I admitted to myself.

After the shock of this morning's episode wore off, we had work to do. We needed to fix the back door that Tristian had busted down in his panic to get to me, and we also had to fix the lock on the garage door. But first things first, I went to make breakfast for us, while Tristian cleaned up the mess from the broken door. As I cooked, I remembered seeing at some point in time a door, and some extra locks in the basement. I wondered if they were still down there. I'd send Tristian down to search. "Wash up Tristian, breakfast is ready" I said with a smile in my voice. It felt so good to have him here. I was reminded of how it was when mom was still with me, and a twang of sadness pulled at my heart for a moment.

"Have I ever told you that you're a good cook Kikyo?" Tristian asked from his side of the breakfast table. "Oh please, it's just bacon and eggs, it's nothing special." I was a little embarrassed I wasn't quite used to the complements he showered on me at any opportunity he had. "No really, I've had other meals prepared by you remember? Anyway, you are a good cook, and will make some man very happy some day with your culinary skills. You know they say that the way into a man's heart is through his stomach, well then I'd say you're golden." He was beaming at me, and looking at me with so much affection, I had no choice but to smile back at him. "Hey if this is your way of inviting yourself, to lunch and dinner, well it worked." We both laughed at that. It was so easy to laugh with Tristian, just like old times. I sure missed our grade school days.

After breakfast, Tristian helped me clean the kitchen, and wash the dishes. I suddenly had a flash forward of my life, we were old and grey, doing the dishes just like we were now, and it was nice. When we were done, it was time to get to work. I had Tristian all to myself for the entire day, and we still had lots to do. "Tristian, I think I remember seeing a door, and some locks, down in the basement somewhere, let's go down and look around, I have some tools down there too." I hated to admit to myself that I was a coward, but I knew that if Tristian was not here with me, there was no way I'd go in that basement to search for anything, I'd prop the kitchen table against the door if I had to.

As we descended the steps down to the dark basement, I was a little too tense and Tristian felt me stiffen up. He gave my hand a gentle squeeze, and pulled me along. "What's wrong Kikyo?" he asked quizzically "Um nothing" I hesitated "It's just that I only come down here when it's absolutely necessary, and I haven't even been on this side of the basement in years. You know that this is where mom found me right?" I was so tense, that I was literally shaking. "Oh, I'm sorry I didn't know" he wrapped his arms around my waist and pulled me closer to him. "It's ok Kikyo, your safe now; I won't let anything bad happen to you ever again." I nodded into his strong chest as I shivered and got myself under control.

The door locks, and tools were all in the far corner leaning against the wall and on shelves. We gathered our supplies, and just as we were about to leave the area, I dropped the box of nails I had. When I bent down to gather up my mess, I caught a glimpse of something glinting in the light cast from the single bare bulb under the shelving unit. "Tristian, hold on a sec." I said just as he was about to turn out the light. I set my cargo aside, and went towards the shelving unit. Beneath the bottom shelve, I found the object of my curiosity, I fished it out, and I turned it around and around in my hand, I knew I had seen this object before somewhere but I knew not where. It was a man's ring. "Tristian look at this" I said as I held it for him to examine. "You think it belonged to the previous owners?" he asked. "I don't know, but I know I've seen it before, you don't think . . ." I trailed off beginning to tremble again form a memory so faint that I could barely make out the edges. "Maybe . . . maybe . . . ugh! Why can't I remember?" he took me in his arms again, shut the light off and led me back upstairs.

We sat at the kitchen table where we both examined the ring again, and again, me in frustration, and Tristian with concern. I was concentrating so hard on the flimsy memories of my "incident" that I started to give myself a headache. "Tristian, amor I don't think I'll ever fully know what happened to me long ago, so lets forget the ring, and get to work." My mood was beginning to sour, and I didn't want to be rude to Tristian, so I shoved the ring in my pocket and we got to work. Once we had the door replaced, we headed out to fix the garage door lock; this was an easy fix that took only a few minutes. I gave Tristian the extra set of keys, to both the garage, and kitchen door that I attached to the key ring that already held the front door keys. I knew that this was a big step giving Tristian all the keys to my house, but I knew in my heart that I could trust him completely. As I handed the key ring to him he smiled at me and said "only as a precaution" and he attached the ring to his own keys.

We were done surprisingly fast with our "home repairs", so we went to take a break, before we got to the real issue at hand. As we sat on the couch, Tristian entwined his strong fingers with mine, and lifted my hand to his lips. He kissed the back of may hand so lovingly, that it made me smile.

I could tell something was on his mind, but it looked like he was having trouble deciding just what to say or how to say it. "Spit it out Tristian, whatever it is" he adjusted himself to be at my eye level, and held my hands just a little tighter as he took a deep breath and centered himself.

"Kikyo, querida, I want you to be absolutely sure of just how much you mean to me. I can't stop thinking about you, during classes, or practice, or when I'm just at home. When I close my eyes, your there on the other side of my lids, when I'm running, your right beside me encouraging me to go faster, and when I'm sleeping, it's like I have you in my arms throughout the night. Kikyo, amor, you are my, for lack of a better word, you're my soul mate; you fill my every gap and make me whole. Now I don't want to scare you off, I know this is soon, we've only just started to know each other again, but you're like the earth, and I'm your moon and sun that orbit's you." All I could do was stare at him, and nod my head as my eyes filled with tears of happiness. When I was composed enough to talk I said "Tristian, I feel exactly the same way. I don't know if were too young to feel this way, but I can't help it and I know it's not just a school girl crush, this is way beyond, how I felt about you back in grade school. Tristian" I paused as I read the look in his eyes "I love you. I love you more every minute of every day. You're the reason I can tolerate to continue living day after day. You're the reason; I haven't let my nightmares literally kill me. I fight my way out those nightmares every night, just so that I can have one more day with you."

"Kikyo, amor, I will love you for as long as you'll have me and beyond. There is nothing I wouldn't do for you. If it's in my power consider it done, and if not, then I'll find a way to please you." Tristian gently kissed my cheek with so much love and adoration, I thought I would burst. I resisted the urge to untie his hair, and let his long locks spill over his shoulders. I knew if I did this, it would only lead somewhere I wasn't ready to go to yet. I ever so gently put my hand on his chest and he understood my gesture. "Let's get to the inevitable work at hand Kikyo" he said tenderly. He knew I was dreading entering mom's room, but it had to be done and I had procrastinated way too long already. "I saw some empty boxes in the basement earlier Kikyo, I'll go get them while you start, or do you want to wait until I come back up?" he asked. "No Tristian, I'll go in and begin, I think I need a moment alone in her room anyway, kind of like a last goodbye. But thank you." He hugged me tight and was off to the dark basement while I stood on shaky legs, and marched to mom's room.

Chapter Four

Broken

I hesitated before the door, and told myself that it was just an empty room. Mom was no longer here and had no need for anything that was left in her room. I took a deep breath, and turned the knob. I flicked on the light and without looking around, I went straight to the window and opened it, the air in the room was stale, and it needed to be aired-out. I stood before the open window (that overlooked the elderly neighbor's walkway halfway between the back and front yards) and started off into space for a moment. I could feel mom in this room, I could almost smell her in this room. I missed her so much it hurt. I nearly jumped out of my skin, when Tristian wrapped his arms around my waist, and kissed the back of my neck. "Oh sorry, I didn't mean to startle you Kikyo, but you looked so lovely standing there with the sun washing over you, I couldn't help myself." I turned to face him, and snuggled into his strong chest, as he caressed my hair, and kissed the top of my head.

"So where do we begin?" asked Tristian "Well maybe we should start in the closet. We'll get all the clothes, and donate it to a church or something." I went into the closet, and began to go through mom's clothes; she had dresses, two piece sets, slacks, blouses and shoes in the closet. I took each item off the hangers, folded them and handed them to Tristian where he placed everything in the empty boxes he had brought up from the basement.

I was actually, calm and very controlled as we worked with mom's clothing for more than an hour. We chatted about nothing in particular, until the closet was almost empty, and then I found a locked metal cash box in the highest shelve, tucked way in the back. "Tristian, look at this" I said as I handed him the metal box. "I wonder what's inside" I said, as he turned it over looking for a key. There was no key attached, so he put it aside, so that we can find a key, or pry it open (which ever came first).

When we were done with mom's closet, we moved on to the dresser drawers. The usual items were stored here, socks, tee-shirts, underclothing, nightgowns etc. then Tristian found mom's jewelry box, I had completely forgotten about it. It was a silver box with engraving on the outside. I never knew what the inscription said as it was in Japanese and I couldn't read it. I think mom had told me once that it was her name, but I'm not sure.

I had never been in mom's room since her funeral, so I had kept the jewelry she wore daily, in my own jewel box. But that was just a simple necklace with a flower charm, a pair of gold hoop earrings and her watch.

Mom's real jewelry was kept put away for special occasions. My hands trembled as Tristian handed me the silver, heart shaped box. I ran my fingers across the scripted engravement, and opened the box. It held mom's wedding and engagement rings, an assortment of gold and silver rings, earrings, charms, bracelets, and necklaces. But underneath all the jumble of jewelry was a single small key. Tristian looked at me and took the key that

We both knew opened the cash box.

"Do you want to do the honors?" Tristian asked as he held out the key and metal box to me. "No, you do it" I said a little shaky, not knowing why my heart was beating a mile a minute. "Ok, here goes". When Tristian opened the box, we found a multitude of documents, house paperwork, car paperwork, birth and death certificates, school records, medical records but at the very bottom of the stack, were the police report of my "incident" and mental health reports. I hadn't realized that I was holding my breath, until I had to gasp for air. Tristian handed me the report, and my hands were trembling so much that I dropped the entire file. "Kikyo, amor, you don't have to read it if you don't want to honey. Do you want me to put away?" Tristian asked as he picked up the mess of papers that had fluttered to the floor. "Um, I think maybe we should finish here before we get to those" I said with an uneven voice. The key to unlocking my Swiss-cheese memory was before me finally, and I was terrified of what information those pages contained.

I was anxious as we hurried to finish in mom's room. We quickly hurried through the rest of the room, and Tristian hauled all the overflowing boxes to the garage. We still had to decide how to distribute the boxes but I'd worry about that at a later date. I refused to look at the metal box that held the contents of my fuzzy memory; instead I went to the kitchen and made some lunch for Tristian. My scars were itchy, as it was warm in the house, and I still wore a long sleeved tee shirt. I knew Tristian wouldn't mind if I changed into something lighter, even if meant he had to see my ugly scars and new scratches. I went to my room to change, while Tristian took the last of the boxes outside.

When Tristian was done lugging the boxes away, I had lunch ready for us on the kitchen table. If we were going to see what my memory was missing, I wasn't going to do it on an empty stomach. I had Tristian wash up and met him at the kitchen table. I hadn't realized just how hungry I was. Maybe it was just the nerves of finally putting the missing pieces of my life back together and stepping back to fully see what I had been unable to remember. We ate in silence, and the whole while Tristian studied my face, and my uncovered neck. It was like we couldn't eat fast enough, but at the same time I wanted to delay the inevitable. After lunch, we both got up still in silence and as I washed the dishes, he rinsed and dried.

"Are you sure you want to do this amor?" Tristian asked as he held me close and kissed the top of my head. "Querido, I can't put it off any longer . . . let's do this." I took a deep breath, and we headed for the dining room table where my past waited to catch up with me.

With trembling hands, I opened the metal box and lifted out the stack of paperwork. I handed half to Tristian, and set the other half before me. Once again I took a deep breath and tried to calm my racing heartbeat. I wondered to myself if Tristian could hear how loud it was beating. I centered myself, and let my eyes scan the pages. I had ended up with the pile that contained birth certificates; mine, moms and even all my dad's papers. I had the wagon's title and the Deed to the house. I had insurance papers, bank information, and even stocks and bonds that I assumed dad had given mom. I'd have to pay a visit to the lawyer that helped me when mom died to see if he could sort all this out as it made no sense to me. I was so engrossed in my pile that I didn't even pay any attention to what Tristian had in his.

I happened to look up when I heard a gasp and saw the look of shock on Tristian's face. He was pale white like all the blood had been drained form his entire body, and he sat rigid on the opposite side of the table. His eyes scanned the pages so quickly I thought it was impossible for him to understand what he was reading. Tristian's lips trembled about as much as his hands, and as I called his name he slowly came back to me, and he let the pages slide from his ungripping fingers, and fall to the table. "Tristian, amor, are you ok? What is it? Can I get you something?" I knew I was babbling, and as I got up to go to his side, he buried his head in his hands and began to sob. I came to him my hands fluttering uselessly, and cradled him in my arms. "Honey, please tell me what happened, what does it say?" he only held me tighter, as he got himself under control and his sobs ebbed. He took a deep breath, and gently pushed me away, so that he could rise away from the table. But as I went to grab for the fallen pages, he took my hands instead and lead me to the living room.

"Kikyo, querida, are you sure you want to know what happened?" he finally said after what seemed an eternity, his eyes full of compassion and hurt. I nodded, and wiped the tears from his eyes. "Tristian, I *need* to know. What was so horrible that you reacted as you did? Please tell me. I can't stand it any longer, and if you won't tell me I'll read it for myself." I was shaking violently from the range of emotions that coursed through me. With complete understanding and much reluctance, Tristian held my hands tightly and filled-in some of the holes in my Swiss-cheese memory.

"The police reports and medical reports say that when your mom came home, she was calling for you, but you didn't answer. She figured you were either outside, or down cleaning the basement. When she didn't see you in the yard, she went downstairs looking for you. All the lights were off, but when she tried turning them on, they weren't just off, the bulbs were all broken. This is when she started to get worried. She kept calling your name, but no answer came to her. Your mom came back upstairs to find the flashlight in the kitchen. When she went back downstairs, she was headed for the tool room, to get replacement bulbs. But when she opened the door to the room . . ." Tristian trailed off like if he was revisiting the scene in his head, then he cleared his throat and shook his head before he continued. "When your mom opened the door, she found you in the farthest corner. You were unconscious; your clothes were all torn, and were covered in blood. But it says in the report that you were pale, and so cold she thought you were dead. You were covered in scratches all over your body, and it looked like you had been severely beaten within inches of death but there was no pool of blood, just what was on your clothes and body." Tristian stopped to wipe the tears from his eyes, and control his emotions. "Your mom ran upstairs to call an ambulance and the cops, but when they weren't there after a few minutes, she went next-door to the right and had that damn guard over there carry you out of the basement and rush you to Norwegian American Hospital in Humboldt Park. She scribbled a quick note for the cops, if and when they showed up to meet her at the hospital. Carlos, that's the guard's name, raced you to the hospital as your mom followed in the wagon."

"Once at the emergency room, Carlos left as the cops arrived only moments later. The doctors say you had lost most of your blood, and it looked like you had been savagely raped and beaten over and over. But from the looks of your hands, you had fought back hard. The doctors gave you several blood transfusions, and ran several tests over the course of the month you were in a coma. They ran tests for STD's, an AIDS test, and even DNA tests to see if they could find whoever did this to you. All the tests came back negative, including a follow-up test that was done a couple of months later for a pregnancy test. Nothing was ever found in the house either, not a forceful entry, or fingerprints, or DNA that wasn't yours. They had you so doped-up that you were essentially a zombie for a month after you awoke from the coma. There are even psychological records that say that you didn't remember anything; it was like your memory had been erased. But in one of the reports your mom says that you had nightmares every night since waking from the coma. The nightmares continued strong for the first year, and then they began to dissipate. Your mom thought you were finally doing well when you were able to sleep through the night without screaming."

"Your mom was so afraid to leave you alone, but she had no choice. She even told the therapist that when she mentioned getting someone to stay with you when she was at work, you went mad. That's when you began to shut down, and even push out your mom. You wouldn't leave your room, and refused to step foot in the basement. But by the middle of sophomore year it looks like things changed, because you started to be more like yourself again. You started to work, and even went back into the basement again. Your mom was so pleased that you had finally left that past behind you, even if you couldn't remember it. The nightmares were all gone, and you even went out with those kids you told me about."

I hadn't said a word as Tristian recounted my tragic story. I went over everything he had said, but it didn't make sense to me. I fought back? I fought back *hard* is what Tristian had said, I was raped repeatedly, I was severely beaten, all this I understood, but what was missing was the reason behind it. The bulbs had been broken, I was left for dead in the tool room, I was drained of most of my blood, but where did it go if all they found was what was on me and my clothes? I mused over this as I chewed unconsciously on my right thumb nail. Tristian was going out of his mind trying to read mine and get a reaction out of me; I just stared off into space, while I tried to remember that night. Nothing was coming to me except the beginnings of a major migraine.

I don't know exactly how long I was lost in thought, but what brought me back, was Tristian snapping his fingers in my face. I came back to the present and focused my attention on the haggard look in Tristian's eyes. He was beside himself with worry, and relief slowly spread across his face, when I reacted to this snapping. "Sorry . . ." was all I could force myself to say. Then the sobs began. Tristian held me tightly to his chest, and stroked my hair and back until I was all cried out and his shirt looked like he had been out in the rain. "Sorry Tristian, I've really ruined your shirt this time" I said as I began another round of sobs. "I was raped?" I asked when my sobs subsided long enough for me to speak again. "I was beaten? Who did this to me? Why didn't mom ever tell me?" I broke off and fought back the next bout of sobs that threatened to begin once again. I blinked back the tears, and took a deep breath to calm myself down. "Tristian, do me a favor amor" I asked in a stronger voice than I expected. "Can you please put all that away and back in mom's closet for me? I need to change and wash up, I've ruined my shirt like I did yours, I'll get you a tee-shirt or something. "Sure honey anything you need" he squeezed my hand and went to put all the reports away.

I went to my closet and found two plain black unisex tee-shirts, one for me and one for Tristian. I left the shirt for Tristian on the back of one of the dining room chairs, and went to the bathroom to clean myself up. I don't know why I didn't shut the door, probably just habit, but I tossed the ruined shirt in the hamper, and I washed my face. I was silently studying the patterns on my arms and my body, when Tristian caught sight of me standing in the bathroom, door open with no shirt on. I didn't even notice him, until his fingers were tracing the scars along with my own. "Kikyo, honey I am so sorry that this happened to you, but at least now we have some answers." He kissed the silent tears that I was unaware of, and handed me my shirt, as he closed the door behind him.

I had the oddest sensation coursing through me, it wasn't quite relief or astonishment, not even numbness, it was just . . . . odd. Like if I had just wakened from a vivid dream, and the memories of it were slowly coming into focus. For once in almost four years my head was clear, and I wasn't afraid to face my demons. When I came out of the bathroom, Tristian was sitting in the living room again, but had turned on the television, I guessed to avoid thinking about what he had learned of me. "Hi" I said when he didn't notice me standing in the archway between the living room and dining room.

"Hey amor, I hope you don't mind I turned on your T.V. are you ok? Do you need anything?" "Tristian honey, please my home is your home, you never have to ask to do anything here ok? And as for me, I'm actually ok. Can you do something for me Querido?" "Sure amor whatever you need" "I'd like to go in the basement again, and see if now I can remember what happened. Will you come with me?" "Kikyo, are you sure you want to do this? I mean of course I'll be with you every moment, but is this what you really want?"

"Tristian, I *need* to do this. I think once I face *that* demon, I can put the others to rest. Please for my sanity's sake, just humor me."

Tristian clicked off the TV and took my outstretched hand and led me back down to the basement to face the horror of my past, right along with me. My hands trembled on the doorknob to the basement door, but I shoved that first fear away, and we slowly descended down the stairs. It was all I could do to keep from running back up, but I held my ground, and took a deep breath. We of course still turned on every light, and avoided the side of the basement with the furnace; my focus was on the tool room, the room that beheld my disgrace. "Kikyo, I'm right here and I won't let go of you, if it gets to be too much, just say the word, and were out of here." Tristian was holding me tight to his chest, and stroking my hair, it seemed he was more afraid of this than I was. "Tristian, I'll be fine really. I know it's gonna be hard, but I have to do this, I've waited too long to chicken out now." "I love you, and I swear to never leave your side. Remember just say the word." I nodded and braced myself for what was to come. Good, bad, or even nothing at all, I was ready. We both crossed ourselves, and together we stepped into my past.

Armed with the knowledge of the police and hospital reports, I was ready for the memories to flood back to me. But at first nothing came. We just stood in the doorway, and nothing. "Maybe we should close the door?" Tristian said in a whisper after we stood there for what seemed an eternity but was probably just a few minutes. I nodded my head, because I couldn't force any words out of myself. We stepped farther into the room and Tristian closed the door behind us. Still nothing came to me, not even a whisper of a memory. "Ugh! This is so irritating! Why can't my brain function like a normal person?" I was so frustrated from being so close I could taste it, and still having those memories a million miles away. "What if we re-trace your steps? Or at least what you can remember? It's worth a try." Tristian still having an iron grip on my hand led me out of the room and back upstairs turning out the lights as we went.

When we were back upstairs, Tristian and I sat at the kitchen table and he had me recount my day, or at least what was still in my hole-filled memory. "Well" I began, "mom had a list of chores for me to do, so I began by doing some homework, and cleaning up here, I had laundry to do, so I took all the clothes in the hamper and the bedding, and tossed it downstairs. I had a few loads to do, so I wasn't looking forward to going up and down all day. But with the first load going, I went out back to do some yard work and when I was done with that like I told you before I threw a pack of frozen chicken in the sink to thaw, then I went back downstairs, to start another load and dust out the basement . . ." I trailed off, as the beginnings of a memory was inching it's way to the surface, I grabbed Tristian's hand and we went into the basement, and as if in a trance, I was back in that August afternoon again. I think I was sub-consciously aware that Tristian was with me, but I was back in that long ago forgotten space in time. I opened the basement door, and flew down the stairs; the lights were already on because when I came down with the first load, I never turned them off. I went to the laundry room, and threw the ghosts of the laundry load into the dryer then put a new load into the washer. I got the broom from a corner in the room, and went to the side of the basement with the furnace. I shied away from the furnace, as usual, and opened the door to what used to be the coal room, mom kept boxes of stuff we never unpacked in there; I turned on the light and began to sweep the ceiling free of spider webs. Next I swept the floor, and when I was done, I swept the area around the furnace and left a pile of dust and webs, in the center of the basement leaving the door open and the light on

With this side cleaned, I had to go to the other side, and clean the tool room. I was uneasy but it had to get done. I was about to open the door and turn on the light when the damn buzzer on the drier went off and scared the hell out of me! I put my broom aside, and went to the laundry room. When I was done, switching the loads, I was about to go back to the tool room, when I heard my name being whispered, "Kikyo . . ." I went ridged with fear, but my feet had a mind of their own and followed the voice, that was in my head, not exactly in the room. "Kikyo . . . Kikyo . . . . I'm waiting for you . . . Kikyo, come to me . . ." that voice beckoned to me and as frightened as I was, that voice was buttery smooth, and it pulled me towards that room. "Kikyo . . . that's right, keep coming, I'm just on the other side . . ." My hand trembled on the doorknob, but I couldn't fight the urge to run, I had to be with that voice, it was still in my head, but at the same time it was in that room. "That's right Kikyo, just a few more steps love, just a few more . . ."

Tristian and I were just outside the room, and my head was spinning, but I kept my equilibrium and steadied my shaking hand on the doorknob. I pulled the door open and was instantly back in my memory. I reached up to turn on the light, but the bulb must've burnt out but I could see a dark figure in the corner with its back to me. "Kikyo . . ." it whispered still in and out of my head, and it's back still to me. I was frozen where I stood, and he slowly like in a dream turned to face me. "Kikyo . . . I've been waiting for you . . . I knew you'd come . . . it was just a matter of time . . . I've been watching you . . . I've been studying you . . . Kikyo, love . . . it's time you join me . . ." when he had turned his body completely to me, I saw those eyes! They were so black and hard, like onyx gems ringed in neon no not neon but blood red! My head screamed at me to run! But my feet were still glued to the floor, and escape was not a possibility. He strode so slowly to me, but his feet never touched the ground, his face radiated a light that made his white skin glow an eerie hue like an aura. I heard the popping of what I assumed were the other bulbs breaking. He took his blood-rimmed eyes from me, and with a slight movement of his hand the door slammed shut behind me. He took another tiny step towards me, and his words filled my head again. "Kikyo . . . I've searched for you for so long, when I found you, I had to have you . . ." My brain was all mush and I couldn't make out what this creature was, his words melted my will, and I still couldn't move. "Kikyo . . ." it was like he was breathing in my name along with the air, and I saw him shiver slightly, he was enjoying this, and I was dumb struck as he held me in place with his eyes.

When I was finally able to form and barely whisper a question, he was still halfway across the room from me. "What *are* you . . . *who* are you?" I asked the figure. "That is no matter love, what matters now is that you are mine, you *will* love me as I you. Now come to me, and tell me you love me . . ." He held out his hand, and shivered again as I took the tiniest step forward. "*What* are you?" Again I asked, this time firmer and louder. Every red alarm and warning siren was going off in my head, but I couldn't escape the magnetic pull he had on me. "Oh, I think you *know* all too well what I am . . ." He said in that same buttery smooth voice. "I'm still waiting for your declaration love, come to me and claim the love I have for you . . ." His eyes fluttered closed as again he inhaled the air around him that carried my scent. "What do you mean to do with me?" I asked in my same whisper as before, realization was slowly beginning to form in my mushy brain. "Love you, is all I want to do. Love you for all eternity. But you must give yourself to me willingly; I will not take what you will not give." "No." I said in a stern voice that surprised even me. "No, I will not come to you. If you are what I think you are, then a thousand times no." My will was returning to me and I took a step back. His lips peeled back from his teeth and I could see his teeth and the fangs that weren't there before grow right in front of my very eyes.

"You will come to me, my love, my exquisite beauty, my Kikyo . . ." My resolve began to fade again when his voice went all buttery once again. Was I seriously arguing with a . . . no I couldn't even form the word in my own mind . . . a *vampire* in my own house? This had to be a dream, I had to wake up. I had to. This was impossible. He took another half step towards me again, and I half-stepped back. I was shaking my head, trying to concentrate on escape. "Kikyo . . . I've followed your life for years now . . . you will *not* make me wait any longer . . . say you'll be my bride . . . say you love me, and I can give you anything you ever wanted . . . Kikyo . . . it's time . . ." this time he took a full step towards me, and my mind cleared enough for me to see that this was real, not a dream. "No . . ." I said weaker this time. "No . . . I will not be your bride. What do you mean you have followed my life for years? Who are you? Why me? The tears began to spill from my eyes blurring my vision. "Enough! Kikyo, you will come to me, we have an eternity for all your questions. But now, the time has come for you to finally be mine completely." "What? No! Get away!"

I turned to finally run from this nightmare, but as I spun on my heels, I crashed directly into his arms . . . impossible he was just on the other side of the room. It was like crashing into a stone wall. He grabbed me in a vise-tight embrace, and then . . . and then . . ." I broke off from my reverie, and Tristian was gripping my hand so tight I thought he would break my fingers. My poor Tristian was sick with the knowledge and worry for me. But I had to finish this. I had to finish this now. I took a deep breath and was instantly back in this long ago horrific nightmare. He pulled his lips back from his teeth and once again exposed the fangs that I knew would be my end. I tried to fight but it was pointless, I tried to scratch his face and gouge out his eyes, but it was like fighting a wall of iron. I could feel him sucking the blood out of me the whole while tearing at my clothes. He forced his stone hard and cold maleness into me again and again, never breaking away from my neck and the vein of blood that supplied him his euphoric stream of blood. I was so weak, but on fire and itchy at the same time. The fire consumed my every fiber, where my blood was sucked out, the fire replaced it, and the itch was unbearable. "Kikyo . . ." he said in my head once again, "Kikyo, you can join me for all eternity, or choose death, I've drained you enough, your to the point of death, now you must choose, but I want you to choose forever with me . . ." "Never" I whispered. I was able to grab a hammer from the shelf above my head, and drive it into his face, before it splintered into a thousand pieces. I heard him wail in furry, and laugh in ecstasy simultaneously.

"Then I guess I must've lost consciousness because that's all I remember before waking up in the hospital." Tristian was holding me so tight I could hardly breathe, it's a wonder I didn't break his jaw, I was trembling so ferociously. Then the inevitable tears and sobs began to rack my entire frame, causing me to convulse like I was seizing. "Let's get you upstairs Kikyo, were done here amor." With that he lifted me like I weighed no more than a feather, and carried me upstairs and laid me on the couch. He stroked my cheeks and my hair with one hand, never letting go of the other. When I was finally under control, I slipped into a deep sleep where I was again in the basement and I was a fly on the wall watching the monster defile me time and time again.

When I awoke, I was still on the couch, and Tristian was still holding my hand, but he had fallen asleep. He was in an awkward position, he was sitting on the floor beside the couch, but his head was on my stomach. I knew he would be stiff and sore, so I just had to wake him. Why did I have to put him through this? I guess it's true, misery *does* love company. I was stroking his long pony tail, when he awoke. "Hey" was all I said to him with a poor excuse for a smile. "Hey back, are you ok?" "Amor, I'm fine, are *you* ok? You must've been so uncomfortable on the floor, why didn't you wake me, or at least let go of my hand?" "Querida, I will never let you go again, and you needed your sleep. How can I be comfortable after what that monster did to you? Is this for real? It's so impossible; I can't wrap my brain around it. Such things just don't exist. But you're so sure that it did occur, we'll get to the bottom of this I swear we will. But *vampire rape*? Who on earth would ever believe this? If it wasn't because I relived it all with you, and I know you couldn't make this up, I wouldn't believe it either. No wonder you repressed it for so long. Honey what can I do to make this better? My darling, I'm here for you, to keep you safe, and to love you forever." "Tristian, I know you love me, and I love you as well more than I can even articulate, just love me forever and that alone will make everything better."

"Tristian what time is it? It must be late; don't you have to go home?" Querida, I called mom when you were sleeping and told her I was staying with you tonight, she understands, it's ok. Anyway it's only seven, not as late as you think." He kissed my hands, and got up off the floor to stretch out. "But what about your dad, won't he be angry? I don't want him to . . . be mad at you or anything." I too got up and had to stretch my too stiff body. "Don't worry about him, mom said he's out with the guys, and he never comes home on the weekends anyway, if for whatever reason he does, mom will just say I'm with one of my friends." "Oh Tristian, please, please don't start lying for me, and especially don't let your mom lie because of me, we both know what he's capable of, maybe you should go, I'll be fine really." "Not a chance, Kikyo love, you can't get rid of me that easy, I let you do it once before, but never again. Hey are you hungry? I think maybe we should go out and eat for a change. What do you think?" His eyes were pleading with me, and I could tell he would never say so, but I knew he needed to get out of this house as much as I did. "Ok, but only if we can go see a movie also, and I promise not to fall asleep again" Tristian's eyes lit up, like I had given him the best news ever. "Awesome! But you might wanna run a brush through your hair first" he kidded, and I swatted at the air when he moved out of the way. "Let me change first love, I need to cover my scars when I'm in public." "Kikyo, please don't think you have to do that for my sake, I bet it's uncomfortable to be so covered up all the time, your fine really." "Darling, it's no biggie for me, I'm used to it, four years of used to it actually, and I'm fine really."

It had been a long day, and I wasn't ready to wrestle with myself concerning the impossibility of vampire reality. I was too tired and wary for that argument. I knew it just couldn't be true, but in my core I *felt* that it was. For Tristian's sake I would let this go, if just for today. I knew he was as incredulous about this as I was, but he didn't seem prepared to take this any farther than I did today. So for now, I would just enjoy my first real date with Tristian.

Back in grade school, dating consisted of doing our homework together, holding hands and talking endlessly about nothing in particular. In all the time I had known Tristian we still had never kissed. Tristian was always careful with and around me. He was always cautious of pushing my limits, and respecting my space. With my mom gone now, Tristian was the only person on the planet who truly understood me, for that alone I owed him so much. "Querida, are you ready?" Tristian called from the other side of my bedroom door. "Come in; just give me a sec. ok?" He entered my room, and sat on my bed as I pulled a brush through my tangled mess of hair, and pulled it into a ponytail. To compromise with Tristian and myself, I opted for a thin long sleeved tee-shirt, instead of my usual turtleneck. When I was done with my hair, I even attempted a little tinted lip gloss, and turned to meet his approving gaze. "Thank You" Tristian said as he rose from my bed and moved to wrap his strong arms around my waist and pull me close. He kissed the top of my head, and led me out of the house on our first official first date.

When we were out of the garage, he asked me what kind of food I was in the mood for; I wasn't really picky so I let him decide. We drove out to same theater out in Melrose Park, and went to one of the many restaurants in the area. The movie wasn't due to start until 9:00 p.m. so we had plenty of time to talk before then. "Can I ask you something love?" Tristian asked when we were done, and were walking back to the car to wait for the time to go in to the theater. "Sure, amor ask away" "Well I've been wondering since that day, what made you call me? Not that I'm complaining or anything, I'm just curious is all." "Oh," I wasn't expecting that question, and had to control the blush that threatened to spread across my face.

"Well, um, do you want the long version or the short and sweet?" "Give me the short and sweet first, then the long detailed version how 'bout that?" "Well, ok. Short and sweet . . . I missed you. I missed you like, the prisoner misses his freedom, I missed you like, a flower misses the rain, and I missed you like I miss my mom. Do you still want the long version" "No I don't think that's necessary, I had no idea. Why did you wait so long to call me? You know I tried calling you a few times, but I guess you were either at work or screening your calls. Either way after a while I guess I just gave up. Funny though how now it's not even weird, it's like we've always been together never apart, and so comfortable with each other." "I know what you mean, we picked up exactly well maybe not exactly, but right where we left off. It's like we belong together or something. Like fate or another higher power gave us the chance to see what it was like to be apart, and brought us back when it was time. Although, life was good to you for the most part wasn't it?"

"Not exactly, it took time for me to come to terms with what you did to me. I went out of my mind when I found out that you were in the hospital. Your mom gave the hospital staff specific instructions, to not say why you were there. Not even my mom knows. All your mom told her was that the house had been broken into and when the thieves saw you, they beat you, and thought you were dead." His eyes were burning into mine, and he was trying to read my reaction in the darkness of the car. "That's what mom told everyone? Oh my God, it must've been horrible for her. No wonder she never wanted to talk about it. All she told me was that when she came home, I was screaming, but by the time she got down in the basement, I was unconscious and badly beaten. She never wanted me know about the rape. They never found who did it, so mom refuse to talk about it. My poor mother would only say that I was "Broken", I guess I know now what "Broken" meant. But Tristian, how is this possible? What if my memories are correct and I feel that they are. Now all of this is making perfect sense to me. All of my nightmares, and the hallucinations when I go running . . ." oops I said too much, I promised myself I wouldn't let Tristian know about the running, damn!

"Running, what do you mean running? What are you talking about?" "It's nothing really, I just run when the nightmares wake me is all, I'm too wired to sleep anymore and I gotta burn off some adrenaline, no big deal." I tried to act nonchalant about the running, but knew I was too much of a bad liar to get away with it. Tristian could read me like an open book, and I knew he wouldn't let me blow this off. "When are you running? Who are you running with?" He asked with a harsh tone, it was the first time ever he ever spoke to me like this and it took me off guard a bit. I knew he already knew the answers to those questions, but I guess he needed me to verbalize it to confirm his answers. "Please" He pleaded in a softer apologetic tone, when he saw me flinch.

I collected my thoughts and had no choice but to tell him the truth. I hated to keep things from him, even way back when we were in grade school, we had no secrets. We knew each other totally and completely, so much so, that a lot of the time we didn't need to converse, we already knew what the other was thinking. "Well to begin with, I know your not going to like this, which is why I haven't told you about it. But also know that since you came back into my life, I haven't been running ok." He was looking at me with those beautiful eyes trying to read what was going on in my head. "Ok. Well you know the nightmares always wake me up right? So it's always like I told you before always at three in the morning. But by the time I calm down enough and realize that it was just another nightmare, I've lost all hope of sleeping anymore. What am I suppose to do at 3 a.m.? So to burn off the adrenaline, I started running. Not far, I only go to Humboldt Park and circle the perimeter, and then I come home. That's all like I said . . . no big deal." I avoided looking into his eyes because if I did I knew the tears would come. "And I assume you go alone right?" he said with a hint of that edge again. He didn't need me to articulate a response this time, when I turned away from him and started out the window this was the only acknowledgement he needed.

"Kikyo, love, alone really? What if something had happened to you? At 3 a.m. it's not safe for you to be running the streets of Chicago. How long had you been running? Couldn't you do something else instead of going out at that hour? Anything could've happened and no one would know." He was hurting again for me; I reached out a hand and caressed his cheek to comfort him. "I tried at first to go back to sleep, to watch TV, to even do homework, but none of that was working. I needed to get out of the house. I know it was dangerous and stupid of me, but honestly, I would rather have taken my chances with the people on the streets at that hour, than going crazy in my house full of shadows and forgotten memories. You know, truthfully though, I think I would've been glad if something had happened to me, then it would all be over. I actually even considered going next door and getting something to "medicate" myself with, or end myself with, whichever came first. But really nothing bad ever happened, I'm ok. Like I said, when you were back in my life, I quit running. Now I had someone to live for, so I've been fighting the shadows, and the broken memories. I've been cleaning, reading, and watching TV, doing homework, anything to kill the time. Please don't be concerned; as long as I have you, I won't be reckless anymore, now I have a reason to stay alive." "Promise?" Tristian asked "Cross my heart" I said as I did actually cross it. "Now let's go before the movie starts without us"

The movie was a comedy that I'm sure Tristian picked in order to get both our minds off of the events that filled the day. It was good to laugh again. Tristian had an arm around me the entire time and I silently wondered if his arm ever fell asleep from the frozen angle it held over my shoulder for the two hours we were in the theater. When the movie was over, he asked if I wanted desert or anything, but I just wanted to get home. I was exhausted from the long day, and needed some sleep. We chatted about the movie the whole way home, and I began to get nervous when we pulled into the garage, and reality hit me that Tristian was going to stay with me the night. I knew he would never dare to overstep his boundaries but it was still very nerve racking to me regardless. I still didn't think it was proper for him to spend the night, but besides his mom who would know?

As I struggled to find my key in my bag, he already had his out and in the lock. It was such a normal gesture that I was already feeling relaxed, until Tristian turned to me before opening the unlocked door, and pulling me tight to him by my waist. "So are you gonna tell me you had a wonderful time and invite me in or not?" He smiled down at me trying again to read what was on my mind. I was blushing a deep crimson red and attempted a smile through my nervous laugh. "I had a wonderful time tonight, would you like to come in for a soda or something?" I was blushing so hard; I thought I would give myself a fever or something. I seriously thought he would kiss me, but when he just kissed the top of my head, I was a little dejected, but he didn't notice. We went inside, and into the living room. I hadn't even noticed before that he had a bag with him, probably some pajamas, toiletries, and a change of clothes. That made it all too real for me, and my blush deepened a shade. I could tell he was amused by my reaction, and he was enjoying my embarrassment . . . what a friend. "So are you gonna get me some bedding or am I sleeping on this couch with no pillow and a blanket?" he asked jokingly when I was staring dumbly at his overnight bag. "Oh, um, yeah sorry, let me get that for you." I shot up quickly, and raced into my closet, to get him a pillow and a blanket. When I came back out, Tristian or his bag was not on the couch, and I guessed he must've been in the bathroom changing. I took advantage of changing as well and calmed the butterflies that were fluttering quickly in my stomach. I hadn't actually planned on where he was going to sleep until he had mentioned the couch, this was just all too real for me and it was going to take some serious getting-used to.

When I came out of my room, to brush my teeth, and finish my nightly ritual, he was smoothing the blanket on the couch. He wore, like me pajama pants and a tee-shirt, but unlike me, he looked ravaging. I could make out every muscle under the thin form fitting shirt, and before I could embarrass myself and begin to blush again, I hurried down the hall to the tiny bathroom. I was brushing my teeth, and still hushing the fluttering butterfly wings inside of me, when Tristian knocked softly on the door and broke my reverie. "Kikyo, amor, are you ok in there?" "Be right out" I said a little too loud in my nervousness. When I came out he was already back in the living room with the TV on channel surfing for something interesting. "So what were you doing in there so long?" he asked with that heart stopping dimpled grin of his as he held his hand out for me to sit next to him. "It wasn't that long Querido, and anyway if you must know, I was calming my nerves" I said looking down at the floor afraid to meet his gaze and blush again. "Nerves, why are you nervous? Do you think I'm gonna take advantage of the situation? I'm only here to do my job ma'am." He said with laughter in his voice and right away put me at ease. "But seriously amor, I will never do anything you are not ready for. Haven't I been a good boy so far, I *can* control myself you know, although when you look as good as you do right now, it takes some real effort to keep my hands to myself." I began to blush again, not as deep as before but enough for Tristian to see, and widen his grin.

I made a move to get up, and Tristian held my hand tighter. "It's still early, stay a while with me" he said as he adjusted himself to embrace me. I stiffened a little, but relaxed when I felt that our heartbeats were in sync and this made me smile. I held him a little tighter than he held me, and I assumed this made him smile as well. After what seemed an impossibly long time to embrace without words, we gently untwined ourselves, and I sat cross legged on the couch opposite of my beautiful Tristian. "So what now?" I asked. I was totally at a blank, and had no idea where the next moments would lead us. "Well you tell me." He said with that same smile that melted my knees, so it was a good thing I was already sitting. "I honestly don't know what do you want to talk about?"

"Can I ask you something?" His posture and his tone had turned serious. "Sure, you can ask me anything . . . what is it?" I was afraid he might want to ruin the evening by talking more about this afternoon's revelations that I had already tucked away in a corner of my brain for later pondering. "I was wondering . . . if . . . you still went to church." He was looking at me intently, and I didn't know what he was trying to get at. "Well . . . um . . . not actually. Mom and I went sometimes to Maternity BVM but it wasn't a regular thing . . . why?" I was taken off guard and a little puzzled by the interest. "Well it's just that I was wondering if you had a Priest or someone like that to talk to since your mom passed. Please, I don't want to be rude or anything, but I can't honestly believe that you haven't talked to anyone besides me since then." His eyes were full of concern again, and I wondered what had brought this question on. "Um . . . no, I haven't talked to anyone professional or anything" I was slightly irritated that he would even hint at something as embarrassing as my needing to talk to someone "*like that*".

"What are you trying to say? You don't believe what happened to me? Geeze, Tristian I don't even believe it, but I *have* to because I know deep down to my core that *that* is exactly what happened. I can't explain it, I can only accept it now, and move on. I've lost too much of my life over this and now I want nothing more than to put it away in some corner of my brain and let my life finally begin. I know that my little bubble was a defense mechanism to protect myself from the outside world, and it truly did help me. I know that it may not seem like that, but when I was essentially a zombie, I may have been only going through the motions, but at least I wasn't hurting enough anymore to the point that I just wanted to end it all. I went on day after day, and I couldn't stand to hurt you, so I pretty much erased you from my life. I didn't want you to have to suffer for me or with me, over something that made no sense. Forgive me but I was weak, confused, frustrated, and angry. Can you understand why I wanted to protect you?"

My little rant must've taken Tristian by surprise because the look on his face suggested that he was amazed I had all this in me. "Kikyo, why would you want to protect me?" He asked in almost a whisper. "Don't you understand that I have loved you since we were kids? Granted it was a different kind of love, but love none the less. I was out of my mind with worry when I went to visit you in the hospital and I wasn't allowed to see you. You gave your mom specific instructions to not allow me in. I tried sneaking in, to no avail. I kept calling the hospital, but they refused to give me more information than the usual stand-by answer: "She's resting, and we'll give her the message that you called," When you came home, I almost knocked your mom out of the way, but I was able to control myself and go away. I was over here every moment I got, and always left frustrated, and confused. It's a good thing we moved because I thought for sure your mom was gonna get a restraining order against me. You say you didn't want to hurt me, you wanted to protect me, well let me tell you something Kikyo Starlita, what you did to me was more hurtful than if you would've let me see you. I didn't care how you looked so long as I knew you were safe and alive." He had to look away from me then; his usual sparkling eyes were tormented and full of the remembered agony that I had caused him so long ago.

"Well now let me ask you a question then Tristian," I was agitated now and the casual mood was long gone now "If I hurt you so bad, then why did you come back when I called you?" It was impossible to believe that it was only a week ago. I was beginning to tremble with the range of emotions building in me, and my traitor tears were forming in my eyes, I blinked them back before they could escape, and increase my ire. "I came back, because even though I had to give you up, I never stopped loving you. You said it before; we're like two puzzle pieces that need each other in order to be complete. We belong together, and this may sound egotistical but I *knew* I'd get you back someday; it was just a matter of time." By now Tristian was as irate as I was, and for some odd reason I found it kind of funny, I began to laugh a little uncontrollably and he just stared at me like I had slapped him silly. "May I ask what is so funny, Kikyo?" he was still staring at me dumbfounded, but the ire was completely gone from his words.

"Throughout our grade school years, you were always at my side, you were my only true friend, and I loved you beyond a doubt. Once in high school I quit you cold turkey and still I loved you. For nearly four years I saw you go from terrified for me, to feeling useless, to utterly sad, then confused as I kept everyone at bay, and finally acceptance. I saw you grow to become the man you are now; from the boy I loved as kids to the man you are now. I saw you become the star athlete we always knew you'd become, I saw you let me go and date all different types of girls, and I saw you actually come to be happy. How could I possibly ruin it all for you? I was, still am in fact the total opposite of you. I let you go because I loved you so much that I couldn't bear to continue to see you waste your life on me. Tristian you have every potential in the world, you have a future ahead of you; please understand that what I did, I did for you." The hysteria had left me, but he still had the look of confusion on his face. "Ok, I get all that Kikyo, but what's so funny about that?"

"Tristian, don't you see? It was all in vain, you never stopped loving me anymore than I could stop loving you. I wasted four years of my life just to keep you away from me, and it didn't work. Even though you led your life away from me, you still kept tabs on me. I know that you called my mom enough not to be a pest asking about me. I know that you still stuck up for me at school, I know that even though you were dating whoever you were with you always compared her to me, to me of all people, why? I set you free to not feel obligated in any way to me. And now we come to the present, you have college before you, and a whole entire life to begin to live after graduation. What can I possibly offer you? I have nothing. You think me so strong, because I haven't ended my life yet. But I got news for you querido; I'm an empty shell, a shadow of my former self. I know you can't believe what happened to me down in the basement, but like I said before, that is what happened. I can't claim to even begin to understand it, but I have to accept it. This is my pathetic life, and I have to get over the facts and move on. You ask me what's so funny about that. It's not funny "Ha, Ha" it's funny as in "incredulous" that after so much time, all I had to do was make one phone call when I was on the brink of insanity, and you drop your entire life to come to my rescue."

"That was never my intention. I was prepared to love you for all eternity or until my life ended, from a distance, but I just had to give in to my loneliness and ruin everything I had worked so hard for. It's not fair to you for me to want you so bad. I can't stand to see you getting involved with me again because I know in the end I'm only gonna hurt you, and I know this time it will be a million times worse. But at the same time, I can't bear to be without you. When I think of all the ways, to let you go again, I just can't do it. It would be like pulling out my heart, or worse my soul and knowing I can't live without either one. I don't want to continue to hurt you, but I need you like I need the air to breath. I long to be with you, every moment of every day, and still if I could let you go once again, I would if it meant that you would find every happiness you deserve out in the world somewhere away from me. I'm too messed up to contribute to you fairly, and it's too much to ask of you to accept me the way I am. I need to find out why this happened to me. What reason on earth could there be for this heinous crime? Could it be possible that the stuff of myth and legend are actually real? I have a quest before me, and I can't ask you to be a part of it. I don't even know where to begin, or what to look for, but like I said, I will not let you throw your life away on me anymore." The hysterics were on the verge of engulfing me and I was trembling so much, the whole couch shook. But when Tristian embraced me tight to his rock hard chest, I lost the conviction in my voice, and sobbed into his chest once again, until the tears ran dry, and I was heaving dry sobs, and trying to get my breathing under control.

"Kikyo, querida, I know you want only the best for me, I understand everything your saying, and despite what you think, I do believe what happened to you was real. But I will not allow you to shut me out ever again. I can't suffer that again. You may not totally understand this, but I love you even more now than I ever did before, I'm with you for the long haul. I couldn't keep you safe before, but now it's different were older and love binds me to you. I will do whatever it takes to keep you safe and happy. So quit trying to end "us" and let me decide what is best for the two of us. You don't ever have to be or do things alone; you can't get rid of me as easily anymore. As long as there is a breath left inside of me, you will be my focus, an extension of myself and my life. Now are you done freaking out for tonight or is there more you gotta get out?" His tone had turned playful again and I was grateful to end this discussion on a good note. Try as I might, it looked like I would get to keep Tristian for as long as I wanted him, or as long as he let me keep him. "Well, I think I'm done for today, but just know that I freak out a lot and just let me know when it gets out of hand and you can't deal with it anymore, I will understand, and I wont hold it against you." He hugged me once more before I got up to go to bed.

Chapter Five

Angel Xavier

Tristian got up to take off the shirt I had soaked with my blubbering, and I had to look away before I began to blush again, but I did manage to gawk at him, my mouth agape and eyes wide, as I took in his chiseled muscular athletic physique. He was perfect, my Tristian put Adonis to shame. I quickly escaped to my bedroom before letting him catch me in this embarrassing moment. As I was turning down my bed, preparing to get in, Tristian softly knocked on my door. "Can I come in a minute?" "Um . . . sure . . . yeah, come in." I stuttered out, wondering what was on his mind. A gasp caught in my throat, as Tristian sauntered into my room. He was still shirtless and looking impossibly glorious. I was beginning to blush, and my heart started to race, as I choked out "What's up?"

"I just wanted to make sure you were ok, and to see if I can get you anything." His eyes were smoldering, or maybe I was imagining it, but either way, his intense look bore deep into my soul, and I had to look away yet again. "Um, I'm good, I don't need anything, do you need anything maybe another blanket or a pillow? Are you hungry?" I kept my eyes averted, but could still feel his gaze on me. "I'm good amor; I just . . . um like I said wanted to make sure you were ok. Will you leave the door open, just in case?" I nodded. Tristian began to turn to go back to his makeshift bed on the couch, when I called him back mid-step. "Um Tristian, can you do something for me?" I asked, keeping my emotions in check. "Sure, anything, Querida, what is it?" "Well, it's just that I was wondering, if you would stay with me until I fell asleep" My words jumbled together as I spoke so fast to get them out before I regretted it and changed my mind. I was looking at his bare chest again, because I just couldn't bring myself to look him in the eye. When did I become so self-conscience around him? Then I wondered if he figured I wanted something more, or if I was just that frightened of my dreams. "Sure . . . let me just turn off the TV and the light, I'll be right in." I had to take a few deep breaths to calm my heart rate that I was sure was off the charts.

Tristian stepped back into my room and gently closed the door behind him. I was already in my bed, and still working on controlling my breathing. I knew this would be an intimate situation, but having Tristian here with me, would ease my nightmares. I was sure of it, now if only I could go through with it, I would be all good. It wasn't like we had never slept together before, but back then we were just kids and our moms let us sleep together when their visits ran long, and we were exhausted of playing all day. But now, well this kind of sleepover was just a tiny bit different than our previous ones.

"Scootch over, Kikyo don't hog the entire bed." I could tell this was Tristian's way of putting me at ease, and lightening the current mood in my room. We were both very aware of each other in the darkness, and I was sure he could hear my heart thumping against my rib cage trying to escape. I jumped a little when he spoke again after a few silent moments. "If you think you can't handle me being here with you, I can be right outside and I'll even leave the door open." He started to go, but I turned over to my side facing him, and touched his shoulder before he could get far. "No Tristian don't go, I'll behave, it's just that well I've never seen you this way before, and it's all just a little startling." I averted my eyes even in the darkness. "Would it make you feel better if I put my shirt back on, even though it is wet, I don't mind." Tristian asked, and I could tell he was getting a kick out of my embarrassment. "No, no it's ok really, just please hold me, and talk about anything so that I can sleep ok?" I was so tired, and even though I was so wound up from the close proximity to Tristian, he held me as I had asked, and I honestly had no idea what he was talking about because I slipped into unconsciousness almost instantly.

I knew I was dreaming, because only in dreams can the things that make no sense in the real world, actually have substance and meaning in the dream world. As I slipped into a deep sleep, I was still sub-consciously aware of Tristian still holding me, I could smell his unique scent, and feel his rock hard chest and arms tight around me. I could feel his chin resting on my head and his breath in my hair. I think I pulled him a little closer and heard a soft chuckle come from Tristian before I was completely gone.

In my dream world, I was in my own house for once; I was back in my long ago day of disgrace. I was going about doing all the same mundane chores that had to be done. It was kind of like watching a film rolling. I went about the day, as I had done with Tristian earlier in the day, but when it came to the point of the day when I was being lured into the dark room, my heart was racing, and I knew what to expect (or so I thought). When I entered the room, the dark shadowy figure was standing with his back to me, talking to me coaxing me inside of my own head. His words were silky, buttery, and warm; there was no hint as to the malice behind them. I stood my ground, frozen in place waiting for the inevitable. As the dark figure turned ever so slowly, I caught his scent in the air, it was vaguely familiar, but my head was fuzzy and I couldn't make it out. When he was finally fully turned facing me, his blood red neon eyes were blazing with a hunger that I couldn't place as bloodlust or just physical lust. I still couldn't move as I was rooted in place beside the open door. He smiled wide and I could see that his fangs were not visible, the flames behind his eyes bore into my very being, and then his face changed, no not changed but I noticed it for the first time ever. All I had ever seen of him before was the magnetic eyes, and the perfect shiny impossibly white teeth.

He was tall maybe 5'8" or so, he was wearing all black, slacks, long sleeved shirt everything was very non-descript. He had long raven black hair pulled back in a tail. His face and hands glowed incandescently from within. His jaw was strong and slightly pointy, his lips ruby red like his eyes and pouty. But besides his extreme beauty, what held my intense gaze was the facial hair, he wore it exactly like . . . Tristian? No! My mind screamed not *like* Tristian . . . it *was* Tristian! When he saw the realization in my eyes, he was instantly inches from my face, I wanted to scream in horror, but his mouth clamped down on mine, and he was kissing me so passionately that I couldn't breath. His arms held me like vices as he pressed his entire body to mine. He contoured to me perfectly, never releasing his lips from mine. I tried to fight back, but to no avail, I might as well have been fighting with a stone wall. Within seconds he had me on the dusty ground, as I continued to writhe under him. His hands were all over my body so quickly; it was like he had more than two hands. He ripped the clothes from my body in one fluid movement, and was about to violently disgrace me, when I was able to reach for an old hammer on the bottom shelve of the tool room, with all my strength, I was able to bash it into his eye. I knew it wouldn't hurt him, but a distraction was all I needed.

He looked at me with a mix of shock, fury, lust and pure evil. He wasn't my beloved Tristian anymore, this being looked nothing like my Tristian. He was still the same but minus the Tristian features, this creature was even more angelic, the opposite of my Tristian but even more glorious. Where Tristian had chocolate brown hair, he was fair haired, he had no facial hair, and his locks were flowing freely, this monster was much more built than Tristian and made him look gangly. And where my Tristian was warm to the touch, this abomination was ice cold. I was about to scream again when he covered my mouth with his hand, and I noticed the ring, he wore a ring made of silver intricately ornate with a red ruby that matched his eyes. I was able to smash the hammer against his back and as his eyes popped, in reflex he let go of my mouth, as I tore the ring from his finger and flung it under the shelving unit as a distraction. His eyes flared once again and smoldered as he positioned himself to do the unthinkable to me. He was laughing as I felt a hard cold stabbing deep within me and lost all consciousness.

"Kikyo, Kikyo! Wake up! Amor, Wake Up!" Tristian was shaking me and shouting at me. He felt and sounded so far away, why was he so far from me? I was in blackness and couldn't tell where he was. His voice was so faint, and I could barely tell he was touching me. I tried to call out to him, but the blackness was too strong, I couldn't speak above a whisper. Then I felt the sharpness against my cheek, it was hard, fast and stinging. "Kikyo, honey wake up!" I could hear Tristian louder now, like the volume on a stereo was being slowly turned up. The darkness was trying to pull me back, but Tristian's voice was pulling me out. If only I could hold on to Tristian's voice I would be able to climb out of this dark abyss. I was steady climbing to meet the urgency in his voice; it kept getting louder and louder. I could feel my teeth knocking together from the force with which he shook me.

My eyes slowly opened and tried to focus in the darkness and safety of the bedroom. I locked eyes with my Tristian and he crushed me to his chest and was kissing my face and head in relief. "Kikyo, honey are you ok, it was just a bad dream. Do you feel ok, do you need anything?" My heartbeat and pulse were calming down and returning to normal. I was taking deep breaths and clung tighter to Tristian as he moved to reach and turn on my bedside lamp. "Are you ok querida?" his voice was so soothing to me. "You gave me quite a fright there for a minute" my throat was so dry I was only able to croak out a quivering "why?" he reached over me again to get me the glass of water I kept on the bedside table. I took a few deep gulps and placed the glass back on the table, then I took one look at my beloved Tristian and a gasp caught in my throat when I saw that he was all scratched, not as bad as I was but his chest was marred by the red welts that criss-crossed his perfect body. I groaned "Oh my God did I do that to you? I am so sorry, please forgive me" "Kikyo, honey it's nothing really, I'm just glad your ok." "What was it like amor, please tell me." I was pleading with my eyes and was a bit surprised that I could actually remember what I had dreamed.

"Well at first, you were ok you were mumbling something about my rock hard chest and perfect body . . ." I was horrified at what I had said in my sleep but he had that grin on his face that melted my knees when he said this and grinned even wider when he saw my blush spread with record speed across my face. "Then after a while, you were making no sense but I think it was an argument with someone because then you started fighting, that's when I was trying to wake you, but you fought even harder and that's when you attacked me . . ." he gestured to his scratches. "but after a few minutes of all the struggling, you went limp, and that's when I worried, I couldn't wake you, and I'm sorry honey, but I had to slap you a couple of times before you came around." I was listening to Tristian re-tell my dream, and remembered the time, "Tristian, what time is it?" I asked. He was still holding me tight and the clock was behind me, well now its 3:15 am, why?" "So that means that once again, I woke at 3 am right? You know this has to mean something, why always 3 am? There has to be some connection between the incident and the time. I will get to the bottom of this . . ." I trailed off when I saw the look in his eyes "sorry, *we* will get to the bottom of this, but now I'm too keyed up to sleep, and this is my unending cycle, the reason I would go running."

"So what have you been doing since you stopped running?" Tristian asked me. "Well . . . I've been mostly stressing until it was time to get ready for school, and zoning out as I tried to watch TV." "So, you never go back to sleep? Aren't you tired?" I gave him a weak smile and shrugged "I am but I'm too wired to sleep anymore, but I guess I can try, will you still stay with me again? At first when I fell asleep it was nice, I was dreaming of you. I can't remember now what I dreamed, but you were there and that's all I need to know that it was pleasant. I'm sorry again that I scratched you up, now we match I guess. But I wouldn't have been so bad if you had a shirt on" I said with a smile and a creeping blush. "Kikyo, amor of course I'll stay with you, come here" he said as he pulled me closer to him, and wrapped his arms tight around me like before, he kissed the top of my head and I nuzzled his neck. I was so tired that to my amazement, I actually did fall asleep again. It was so comfortable in his strong arms, and his scent lulled me to sleep.

I awoke to the smell of bacon, toast and coffee, my stomach rumbling so loud that I was embarrassed Tristian would hear. Was I dreaming the smell of the food? As my eyelids fluttered open, my hand was reaching for Tristian, but he wasn't anywhere in my room, I guessed the food wasn't a dream after all. I looked over to the clock on my bedside table and read out the time but had to look again to make sure the time was right. The red digital readout numbers said it was 10:35 am. Had I actually slept late for the first time in over four months, I couldn't believe it. I woke up feeling oddly energetic, and content. I got up and stretched, before making my way into the bathroom. I snuck into the bathroom, smiling to myself as I heard Tristian in my kitchen humming to himself. I quickly took care of business and washed up, so that I could face the day with a new perspective. When I was done, I lightly stepped into the kitchen where Tristian was busy setting the table. "Good morning sleepyhead" he chimed with a big grin. "Good morning Tristian, what's all this?" I asked gesturing to the spread he had set on the kitchen table. "Well, why do you always have to be the one who cooks? I *can* cook too you know." He said with that same beaming smile of his. "Now come and sit down, eat before it gets cold." "Thanks, Tristian. I really mean it." I said as I took a sip from my cup of coffee.

"So what's on the agenda for today, amor?" I asked between bites of my breakfast. Tristian was eyeing me with carefully, and I could tell he had already set plans in motion for us today. A sheepish little smile began to spread across his face, making his eyes twinkle. "Well . . . um . . . I was hoping that we could go to church today." His eyes never left mine, and I suppose he was weighing my reaction to this, as he said it. "Um . . . ok . . . . I guess if you really wanna go. Which one? You know I don't really belong to any church, but I guess we could go down the block to Maternity B.V.M." I gulped down some coffee and saw his smile spread even bigger. Questioningly I asked "Did you not want to go there, it's ok, wherever you wanna go." "Yeah, B.V.M. is fine, it's just that well, I was kind of hoping that my mom could join us." "Your mom, uh yeah I guess that's ok, but, no offense, but why?" "Well mom's been worried about you too, and she knows I've been spending all my free time with you, she wants to see you again. If it's not cool, it's ok; she'll understand you're not ready for that yet." His smile had faded, but his eyes still twinkled. "Well what time is mass?" I asked Tristian, as I made up my mind to let one other person into my much too complicated life. "Spanish mass is at 1:00, I guess we can get dressed, and pick up my mom at noon. You'll make her very happy. Thanks for this Kikyo; really, it means a lot to us." He came around the table and kissed the top of my head. "Now finish up, I'm gonna take a shower if you don't mind."

After Tristian left the kitchen to shower, I began to clean the kitchen; there wasn't much to clean because Tristian had cleaned as he cooked. All

I really had to wash were the dishes, utensils and cups we had just used. I was worried about what to were, and what to say to Mrs. Garcia, but I guess I would stress about that later. I hadn't been in church since my mom passed away, and even before that we didn't really ever go. As I was looking in my closet deciding which dressier blouse would conceal my scars best, I put away all of my newfound knowledge, all my fears, and all of my nightmares, for later tonight when I wouldn't have the safety of Tristian's arms to protect me tonight. I was hoping that I would be able to recall the memory of the safety he offered when I needed it most.

I finally decided on a brand new thin long sleeved mock-neck ice blue silk blouse that mom had given me for a birthday a few years back, and black trousers. After making my bed, I laid out my clothes, and turned only to run smack into Tristian as he was casually leaning in the frame of my open door. "Oh . . . sorry, amor, I didn't see you there." I had to once again catch a gasp in my throat when I saw just how utterly impeccable he looked. Tristian wore a thin, light tan cashmere sweater over a white button down collar shirt and perfectly pressed khaki pants. He laughed gently as he caught my hand and pulled me to him, to embrace me and kiss the top of my head once more. My heart raced at the close proximity to him, and the unbelievably heavenly scent radiating from his body. I would have to remember to ask him what cologne he used. I had to pull away, if I wanted to keep my senses about me, and not do something I wasn't entirely ready for. Tristian felt me stiffen, and relaxed his hold on me and let me by. "Take your time, amor." He called after me as I stumbled down the hall to the bathroom.

I took a quick shower and then dried my hair to attempt to do something to it. I usually just let it air dry and left it either loose or in a pony tail. But for today I decided to at least try to do it a little differently. I felt that I looked plain enough by Tristian's side, so a little product in my hair and maybe even some light makeup wouldn't kill me. I did the best I could with a loose up-do and some mascara and tinted lip gloss. I had to admit, when I was done, I didn't look terribly horrible as I thought I usually did. When I came out of the bathroom, still wrapped in the towel, I had to race to my room to get dressed. After fumbling with the buttons on the back of my neck, I gave up and headed for the living room to have Tristian help me close the uncooperative buttons. I had to stop short when I saw the look on Tristian's face. He eyed me from head to toe, and before

I could stop the blush that blossomed all over my body, he was up off the couch in an instant and held me tight to his body.

"Wow, Kikyo honey you look absolutely ravishing!" Tristian held me at arms length to look at me with gloriously approving eyes. "That color becomes you. I will be the envy of the congregation at B.V.M., when they all see the beautiful girl on my arm." He kissed the top of my head once more careful not to muss it and squeezed my hand, as I unfolded myself from the embrace he held me in again. "Thanks" was all I could get past my lips. I was so self conscience all the time and lately even more so when I was with Tristian. "Amor, can you button me up please?" I asked as I turned my back to Tristian. After he did up the buttons, I felt his fingers linger at the nape of my neck, and I shivered as the electricity traveled throughout my entire body. We needed to get out of here before my will crumbled and all hope of restraint was lost. "Ready querido?" I asked as I turned and met his piercing gaze. "Wouldn't want to keep your mom waiting." With that we both came to our senses and headed for the back door.

During the drive to pick up Sra. Garcia, Tristian held my hand, and kept glancing at me out of the corner of his eye, until I insisted he keep both eyes on the road. He smiled at me and squeezed my hand before obliging. My stomach was doing flip flops, as we approached Tristian's house. I had never been to his house, Tristian had moved from my block sometime during freshman year. Tristian Sr. worked for a law firm as a paralegal, and Sra. Garcia was now a stay at home mom, since her husband was earning a good salary and was able to afford a nice home in a neighborhood near school. It was a beautiful house. All the window boxes held perennials of all colors, the lawn was impeccably manicured, and the wrap around porch was easily inviting. I was intimidated as we walked up the path to the front door. Tristian had an arm wrapped around my waist, and encouraged me up the stairs, with a beaming smile.

Sra. Garcia was in the open doorway, before we even made it all the way up the stairs. She had her arms open ready to embrace me. Tristian let me go and I went willingly into the arms of my mom's best friend, and hugged her as tightly as if she were my own mother. "Kikyo, hija, how are you? It's so good to see you again. My my, don't you look beautiful, come in come in. Tristian, go call your father he's in the yard." Tristian went around the side of the wrap around porch to get his father from the back as his mom pulled me into the house. "Hija, how are you really? Tristian tells me you've been having a hard time lately? Is there anything we can do for you?" "Oh, Sra. Garcia, you've done more than enough for me just by letting Tristian spend so much time with me. I do hope I didn't cause any trouble by asking him to stay. It's just that I've been so alone for so long now that I really needed someone to talk to and someone to help me clean out mom's room. I know I couldn't have done it alone. I hope you can understand." "Of course, dear. Don't you worry yourself one bit. I've never seen Tristian so happy. It's like your doing us a favor, not the other way around. Look, I loved Rosario like a sister, and I promised her that I would look after you as best I could. I fear that I haven't really kept up on my promise, but I want to make it up to her. If you think that Tristian's being with you is helping in any way, then by all means, don't stop a good thing. But do remember that school comes first okay?" "Of course, Sra. Garcia, I understand and thank you . . . for everything."

"Well, well, well, if it isn't little Kikyo . . . how are you kid?" Sr. Garcia, put his hand out for me to shake it, but when I extended my own hand, he pulled me up into a surprising embrace. I wasn't used to much physical contact, and so I stiffened slightly hoping he wouldn't notice. I inconspicuously sniffed his shirt to see if he'd been drinking, but when I didn't smell anything but fabric softener, I relaxed and hugged him back. "Sr. Garcia, it's so good to see you again, I hope you're well?" He released me and patted my shoulder. "I'm good, thanks. So you kids are off to church with Lupe I hear? Well that's good. Have fun and see you around." Sr. Garcia was a few paces headed back to his yard work when he turned around. "It's nice that you kids are together again, please don't be a stranger. Lupe, don't worry about dinner, Tristian, not too late tonight, Kikyo, see you kid." Then he was gone, and I was able to relax again. It always made me nervous when I was around Sr. Garcia. I knew what he was capable of, and I had seen him drunk before, but he seemed well and Tristian hadn't said anything about his drinking, maybe he was under control now. I hoped so.

"Bye Pop. Ladies, shall we?" Tristian led us out of the house. When we got to the car I was surprised that Tristian put me in the front with him and his mom in the back seat. I didn't say anything but they exchanged a look that sent me lightly blushing. Sra. Garcia talked non stop about how she had promised to keep an eye on me, and how she had failed my mom. I kept insisting that she not beat herself up about it. In truth, even if Sra. Garcia had tried to make good on her promise, I probably wouldn't have let her anyway. I told her it was okay and that now Tristian was looking after me. I thanked her again for her understanding, and for her compassion. Tristian was silent the whole ride to the church and never once let go of my hand. Once we were by the church, parking was hard to come by so Tristian let his mom off in front and he and I went to look for a space to park. "Save us a seat mom, we'll be right in." Tristian called after his mom, who nodded and smiled at us.

We found a spot about a block away, and walked hand in hand to find his mom, saving us space in one of the back pews. I wasn't very religious, so it was kind of hard for me to follow along, all I understood was that the sermon, and the Gospel reading centered around grapes. Either way, as long as I was with Tristian, that was all that mattered. Once mass was over, Tristian left Sra. Garcia and I in front of the church and was off to get the car. We went back to Tristian's house to drop off his mom, and then headed back to my house. I was feeling kind of bad that Tristian was driving so much between our homes, but what else could we do? Tristian didn't want me driving my wagon because he thought that it was in such bad condition that it would eventually leave me stranded somewhere. We would have to compromise on our transportation situation but somehow I felt that was going to be a losing battle. It was still early evening when we were back at my house, so I asked Tristian what he wanted to do as I threw some cubed steak and fresh vegetables in the pot and set it on low. "How about we watch a video?" He asked as he headed for the living room. My selection of movies was so out of date, that I doubted he would find anything suitable to watch.

When I was done in the kitchen, I came to the living room to find Tristian had actually found something that wasn't too outdated to watch. It was a comedy that would have us both in stitches and take our minds off of the true reason we were both looking for distractions. "Querido, can you help me undo these buttons please, I want to take this blouse off before I ruin it." Once again when Tristian was done with the buttons at my neck, his fingers lingered longer than necessary and sent the electric current scattering through my entire body. I thanked him and went to my room to change and get more comfortable. As I was changing into my usual tee shirt and jeans, I wondered what my night would be like without Tristian to scare away my nightmares. I shuddered to think what would've become of me had Tristian not been in my life again. I jumped out of the reverie I was in when Tristian softly knocked on my door and asked if I was okay. "Be right there amor." I said as I collected myself and took the pins out of my hair and let it loose.

Tristian played with my hair, twining it through his fingers again and again as we watched the movie. Tristian's happiness was contagious, and I was laughing right along with him. How long had it been I wondered since I truly laughed. Being with Tristian was comfortable, it was just so right. We were like two grade school kids again, and it felt so good, to just let myself go, and not jump at the slightest shadow that I *thought* had moved. When the movie was over dinner was ready and Tristian set the table, as I served the stew. We both knew that he would be leaving soon, and we made the best of it. Conversation was light and after dinner, Tristian helped me clean up before he had to go.

"Kikyo, querida, are you gonna be alright? Promise me you won't go running if you wake up early. And don't turn off the phone. Honey I don't want to go, but you know if I had any other choice I would stay. Don't leave the house for anything, I'll be right here to pick you up tomorrow morning for school okay? If you need anything, anything at all, please, please, please call me right away. I love you." Tristian was crushing me to him so tightly that I could barely breathe, but in his desperation to keep me safe, I could overlook the momentary lack of oxygen. I was just as desperate to oblige and I loved him just as much if not more than he loved me. We clung to each other for a while longer, but with more relaxed grips. All we could do was pray that I would get through this night, in one piece. He kissed the top of my head, my eyelids, my cheeks, and lingered just above but never touching my lips, when I automatically stiffened. He let me go then, and kissed both my hands, and was out the door. "I'll call you from the car Kikyo."

I saw him drive out of the garage, and ran back inside the house to catch the phone on the first ring. Tristian chattered the whole drive home about how happy his mom was to see me, and how happy it made him to see me looking happy and laughing again. I was floating on cloud nine the entire day I was with Tristian, but now, my cloud had begun to darken, at the thought of the nightmares that awaited me once I had to give over to sleep. I tried to put all that out of my mind, and went about collecting my things for school tomorrow. I made sure I had everything in my bag, and then I went about looking for something to wear. I had the sneaking suspicion that something new and exciting was on the verge for me very soon. When Tristian was finally home, we said our goodnights, but not before he made me promise once again, to call him for whatever reason, and to not under any circumstances leave my house until he came for me the next morning.

I stalled as much as I could, but I eventually had to get ready for bed. I went into the bathroom, washed the make-up off my face, and brushed my teeth. I changed into my pajamas, and went to curl up in my bed. It felt so empty and cold without Tristian to hold me and keep me safe. I set my alarm for 6:00 am, something I hadn't done since my nightmares began. I guess it was just wishful thinking that I would sleep through the night, and just might need an alarm to wake me at the appropriate time. I don't know if it was that I was in church today or that Tristian had stayed with me Saturday night or even that I was in a positive state of mind, but something led me to get down on my knees on my bedside, and say a prayer, for salvation. I prayed for salvation from myself and on-going happiness for Tristian. I felt happier than ever, with this newfound emotion. I could still smell Tristian on my pillow and sheets. I drifted off to sleep with the memory of Tristian's arms wrapped tightly around me, and his lips inches from my neck, as we slept last night.

I was jolted out of my sleep, when the loud shrill of the alarm buzzed repeatedly in earnest for me to wake. I was disoriented and not quite sure I understood the meaning of the buzzing. But as the confusion slowly crept into realization, I was up in a flash. I turned off the annoyingly loud buzzer and stretched the rest of the grogginess from me. It was six in the morning, and I had made it through the night. I couldn't remember if I had dreamed at all. But this was good, this was very good. I quickly got up and rushed about. Tristian would be here in half an hour and I had to hurry. I hastily made my bed and ran to the bathroom to take a ten minute shower. I ran a brush through my hair, dressed and had five minutes to spare. I grabbed a granola bar and ran to the front porch where Tristian was just pulling up in front of my house. I ran down the steps and flung myself into his waiting arms, as he held the car door open for me.

"Did you have a good night Kikyo?" Tristian asked after taking stock of my mood and expression. "Oh, Tristian, it was wonderful. I don't even think I dreamt. Guess what, I actually had the alarm wake me this morning." We both wore matching grins of happiness. He closed my door, and came around to get into the car. He immediately took my hand, and we were off to school. "So why do you think last night was different?" he asked as we drove to school. "I'm not sure really, it must have been the great weekend I had with you." I was a little embarrassed to admit that it was my memory of him holding me all night that got me through my sleep. I was feeling very good, and so I had decided that I needed to go back to work. I knew that Tristian would have practice after school also, so it would work out fine. I cleared my throat to get his attention and voice my thoughts.

"Tristian, I think I'm ready to go back to work. I'll call my boss Steve during lunch and see if I can start today, and I'll let you know after school. You have practice today right?" "Are you sure you're ready to back to work? Isn't it too soon?" I knew he was just concerned about me, but I sort of felt that he didn't want me to work for a different reason, but I let it go. I felt good today and it was the beginning of a new week and a new me. "We'd better get going if were gonna make it to class on time. I'll see you by my locker after school and let you know what Steve says." I reached up to hug him and he whispered in my ear that he loved me. Tristian hugged me back and kissed the top of my head. We headed off in opposite directions to our respective classes.

Home room was the first "class" of the day. After stopping by my locker for the books I would need to get me through my morning classes, I headed for my home room. I felt a little awkward as I hurried to my seat in the back corner of the class, as all eyes were on me. I guess by now everyone knew that Tristian and I were together. A couple of girls that I had actually known since grade school came over to my desk with incredulous smiles plastered to their faces. "So, Kikyo is it true that you and Tristian are a couple now?" the one that asked was named Kim, she was short and thin, like her hair, with no real shape to her. The girl with her was kind of her shadow, and had been since grade school. Veronica was tall and not really chunky but just kind of thick. She wore glasses that didn't really fit the shape of her oily face. I was kind of startled considering that in the entire time I'd known them we had probably spoken only a handful of sentences. "Um . . . yeah . . . I guess we are." I answered and smiled sheepishly, as I blushed. "Wow . . ." said Veronica in unabashed wonder. "Well good for you, it's about time you snapped out of that morbid mood you've been in for the past four years." She was about to say something more, but Mr. Kotwazinski, came into the room and called home room to order.

Mr. Kotwazinski, was half-way through taking roll call, when he was interrupted by a student that walked in late and handed him a slip of paper announcing him as a returning student. Mr. Kotwazinski took the slip and directed the new (to me) student to the only empty seat left in the room, which happened to be right next to mine. "Everyone, for those of you who haven't met him before, this is Angel Xavier San Salvador, Mr. San Salvador welcome back to Steinmetz. Now where was I, oh yes, Mr. Tyrone Lambert . . . "Present" Mr. Lambert, I see you have detention again this entire week I'll save you a seat. Miss. Janet Madigan . . . "Present" Miss. Kikyo Martinez . . . "Present" Now Miss. Martinez, you look well, is that a smile?" I blushed with embarrassment. I hadn't known I was smiling like an idiot, and I quickly cast my eyes to my desk. Mr. Kotwazinski continued like this until he completed his roll call.

I unconsciously doodled in my notebook, as I daydreamed out the window. Mr. Kotwazinski droned on about the upcoming graduation, and deadlines for this or that. I nearly jumped out of my skin when the new boy "Angel" touched my arm. "Sorry, I didn't mean to startle you, I'm Angel and you are . . . ?" "Um . . . oh, I'm Kikyo, nice to meet you." I put my hand out to shake his, but he didn't offer his hand, so I let mine drop to my desk self-consciously. He was staring at me with an odd look in his eyes. I turned my head to look out the window and continue to daydream, but I could feel his eyes burning into me. I whipped my head around to ask him what his problem was but before I got the chance to say a word, the bell rang and Angel Xavier was out the door in a flash.

I hurried on to my first actual class of the day, with horrible Mrs. Browning teaching algebra. Math was not my friend, but since I had no social life up until Tristian re-entered my life, I studied a lot and was able to scrape by with fair grades. I honestly tried to concentrate, but my mind kept wandering back to Tristian, and the way the new boy Angel had stared at me. When math was mercilessly over, I headed off to Spanish with Mr. Rivera. Spanish, I had only taken to get an easy "A" and fulfill my language requirement. English was next on my schedule with Mrs. Mertleman. I had to stop short when I entered English, and saw Angel Xavier, in my class. I hurried to take my seat next to Angel Xavier. "Kikyo . . . right . . . what a surprise to have this class with you and get to sit next to you again." When he spoke I couldn't resist the sound of his voice. He flashed a brilliant smile at me that left me quite stunned. His voice was low and buttery almost musical. "Um . . . yeah, what a coincidence." Was all I could get out before Mrs. Mertleman began class; it really was strange, he continued to stare at me like he did in home room.

Angel Xavier, went to have his slip signed, and once again came to sit next to me. I had never noticed before that I usually had at least one empty seat around me. My anti-social behavior had led everyone to avoid me in all my classes. Angel Xavier; was saying something, but I was off daydreaming about what my future held for me. We were starting to read "*Ibsen*", and everyone groaned when Mrs. Mertleman announced that we would have to pair off and write our final paper on one of his four great plays. Before I could even finish my groaning, Angel Xavier was already calling me "Partner". I could tell already that Angel Xavier was going to get on my last nerve very soon, if I had anymore classes with him. Again he stared at me, and I sighed as I knew that if I said anything, embarrassment would inevitably follow.

"Kikyo, don't worry about the paper, I've done *Ibsen* already, so this will be no problem for us." Something about the way he said "*us*" made me feel uncomfortable. Since having only broken out of my bubble just recently, I was having a hard time, with all the attention that Angel Xavier, and all the mute eyes around me were directing towards me. Angel Xavier was nice enough, but something wasn't quite right about him, I couldn't put my finger on it, but it was something all right. After English, I asked Angel Xavier where he was headed next; this time it was on to History with Mr. Spintz and once again the seat next to mine just so happened to be empty. "You know, if I didn't know any better, I'd say you were stalking me, Angel Xavier." I tried to sound casual, but I know there was a hint of nervousness in my voice. "Please just call me Angel." He said in that buttery voice, and with a smile that could melt an iceberg.

After class, I had to get to my locker, and exchange books. Angel walked with me to do the same. It was no surprise that his locker was across from mine, on the opposite side of the hall. When I saw the physics book he carried, I didn't even bother to ask what his next class was. He followed me to Biology with Mr. Burbulys as his physics class was right next to mine. All the way to class, I caught snippets of conversations going on, with me as the topic. I heard things like, "I wonder what Tristian has to say about this new guy with Kikyo" and "Did you know they have had Homeroom, English and History class together so far?" and even worse "ever since Kikyo, came out of her bubble, suddenly she has the two most gorgeous guys in school following her around, it's so not fair!" Oh the horror, to have to face two more months of this before graduation set me free from this torture. Angel, walked beside me, and glared at everyone enough to make some of them wince, and then softly chuckled under his breath.

Biology was uneventful, and Mr. Vargas was passing out a pop quiz when I entered. Everyone turned in their seats in time to see me blush as Angel Xavier left me at the door and went on to his class. I had to bury my face in my hands when I got to my seat. I put my blazing cheek against the cold black top of the lab table. This was going to be a long two months. I was looking forward to lunch, where I could get away and escape to the ladies room and know that Angel could not follow me there, but I did have to call my boss and see if I still had a job to come back to. When Angel met me at the door, I turned to him stopping in the middle of the hall, "Don't tell me, you have lunch next?" I wasn't really mad, but it was just not right that we had overlapping schedules all day and if we didn't have a class together, we were surely going to run into each other in the hall during class changes. "We'll, I guess I kind of do. How strange." He said it so off-handedly that it probably was just a coincidence, after all he had transferred here so late in the year, and all my classes had available seats for him. Still the look in his eyes didn't convince me. It was like he was holding out on some secret and I wasn't allowed an inside look at it.

I put my books away, when we were at our lockers again, and hurried off to the pay phone by the cafeteria. Almost everyone in the school had cell phones, so I was lucky enough to not have to wait for a phone. I quickly dialed my boss's number and asked if I could come back to work. Steve was happy that the time off had a good effect on me, and told me I could come in next week, to take an additional week off so that the girl he had replaced me with could be re-located somewhere else. I thanked him, and hung up the phone to leave Tristian a voice message on his cell phone. I let him know that I wouldn't go back to work until next Monday and to meet me by my locker after school. I nearly smacked into Angel if it weren't for his outstretched arms, ready to fend me off, when I spun around, and was headed for the ladies room. "Aren't you going to eat lunch Kikyo?" Angel asked with those smoldering eyes. I couldn't escape now. I sighed and followed as he led me into the crowded cafeteria. It seemed all eyes had turned to stare at us as we entered and stood in line to get some food. I wasn't actually hungry, my stomach was doing some weird acrobatics and I was afraid if I ate anything, I would probably regret it. I opted for a lemon-lime soda, in hopes that it would calm my stomach. Angel seeing that all I took was a soda did the same. He insisted on paying, since as he said I had been nothing but friendly to him so far on his fist day back.

We sat at an empty table in a far corner of the cafeteria across from each other. I opened my soda and took a sip to settle my flip-flopping stomach. "So . . . where are you from Angel, tell me about yourself." I asked, actually very interested. "I just moved back here from the western suburbs actually. My father is a stock broker and my mother is a private school teacher, she works with autistic children. Their actually divorced now, so I moved here with my father. He's rarely home, and that gives me the freedom to come and go as I please." He said this with a mischievous grin that was sending many red flags through me. "Oh, I'm sorry about the divorce, are you close to your dad?" I asked "Not really, but like I said, I have the freedom to do as I please, and he doesn't really care either way. My mother is also so busy with her kids that she's oblivious to the fact that I was even there. But it's all worked in my favor. They both make good money and I don't have to work, they are so guilty of the fact I pretty much raised myself that they bend to my will, whenever I want." I couldn't really tell if what he was saying was true, but what was it to me? "Well, I guess as long as you're happy, that's what matters right?" "Yes, as long as I'm content, that's all that matters." He said this with an edge to his tone, that made me draw back a bit, not really realizing that I was leaning into him, he spoke so low that I had to strain against the noise of the cafeteria, just to hear him clearly.

"So, now you know about me, tell me about yourself." He folded his hands over his unopened soda can, all the while his eyes trying to read my soul. I had to stammer, before I could get any coherent words past my lips. "Well . . . um . . . I guess . . . my story, isn't really all that interesting." I finally got out. "My dad, died before I was even born, my mom raised me on her own. My mom died about half a year ago, and now I've met you. That pretty much sums up my life." The entire time I had to look down at my can of soda, so that I would avoid losing myself in his odd violet eyes. "I think there's something you're not telling me" he urged. Why was I compelled to tell this stranger anything about me at all? I had just met this boy today, and already he was irresistible to me. It was like he was a magnet that I could not escape from. His violet eyes, held mine until I broke away and glanced around the cafeteria, and saw to my chagrin; most of the cafeteria was staring at us. Thankfully, lunch was just about over and people started to mill about and dump lunch trays, and start going to retrieve books for the afternoon classes. "I think we'd better get going too, or we'll be late for next period." Angel agreed with a slight nod, never taking his eyes off me.

After lunch, Angel Xavier was off to math and P.E. was next for me, I wasn't really an athlete, but my past few months of pre-dawn running, had made me much more agile. I didn't really understand the point of dodge ball, but at least I was quick enough to get out of the way, even if I couldn't throw hard or well enough. When P.E. was over, I ran to quickly shower and change. I always wore a long sleeved tee shirt under my gym shirt, to cover my arms. I was ever so grateful for all the one person shower stalls; we thankfully did not have one giant communal shower like in the movies or other schools. It was bad enough that I was always so self conscious, but to be able to keep the worst scars to myself was a God-Send.

Being a senior and having so many extra credits as a result of my self-imposed exile into my own private bubble, I didn't have anymore classes after P.E, so I figured I was free from Angel for the rest of the day. I was wrong. When the day had ended for me, I walked to my locker and my waiting Tristian, and saw Angel already at his. I was slightly alarmed to see the intensity with which Angel glared at Tristian. Tristian, didn't notice Angel, he only had eyes for me. Tristian casually leaned against my locker, and opened his arms wide enough to enfold me in them. He kissed the top of my head, and made me blush. "I have missed you every minute we've been apart Kikyo." Tristian cooed into my ear. "Amor, I've missed you too." We still clung to each other, and only broke our embrace, when Angel slammed his locker shut, and stalked off furious. "Did, I miss something?" Tristian asked bewildered. "That was Angel Xavier Salvador, he's new, well not new but back, I wonder why he was mad. We have a few classes together, and he seemed ok all day. Well anyway, I talked to my boss Steve, and he said that I could start again next Monday. Do you have practice now, I can take the bus?" I was gathering my books, for my homework, and hoping that Tristian was free tonight. "Yeah I have practice but, I want you to take my car, I'll get a ride from one of the guys, and I'll see you later for dinner is that ok?" "You want me to drive your car?" he was already taking my hand to place the keys in them, and kissing my forehead, before I could argue any further. "I'll see you around six." He kissed my hands, and was off, muttering something about thinking he recognized Angel or something like that.

I walked out to the parking lot, to find Tristian's car and go home. I noticed that Tristian had taken my house keys off the ring, and gave me only the car keys and his house keys. I smiled secretly to myself, at this tiny show of love from Tristian. I wondered if I should go home and switch cars, or just go in his to pick up some much needed groceries. I didn't want anything to happen to his car, but then I would lose time, and not have dinner ready if I went home first. I drove out to the grocery store that was on the way home from school. It didn't take me long in the store; I was never an enthusiastic shopper. Whenever I went shopping, I would get what I went for and get out as fast as I possibly could. With my shopping done, and the groceries loaded into the back seat of Tristian's car, I headed home at last.

Once I had the car in the garage, it only took me two trips to get all the provisions in the house. While dinner was cooking in the oven, I started my homework, but couldn't really concentrate. My thoughts kept creeping back to Angel Xavier. He was the only other person, besides Tristian who had had such an extensive conversation with me ever. I kept going back to the fact that Angel Xavier and I had some classes together. I was replaying in my head, his reaction to Tristian at the end of the day, and how he seemed overprotective of me, almost territorial. How strange that this new boy would shake my foundation so profoundly. I tried my hardest to concentrate on my homework, but it was no use, I was too intrigued with Angel Xavier. Every time I closed my eyes, I only saw his violet eyes staring intently into mine. I realized that I didn't even know what the rest of him looked like; I hadn't noticed anything besides his deep violet eyes. I wondered why he had chosen violet contacts, and what color his eyes really were. I couldn't even recall the color, length, or texture to his hair. Only his hypnotic eyes were imprinted on my brain.

I nearly jumped three feet out of my skin, when I felt a strong embrace, and lips kissing the top of my head. I spun out of my seat swinging and caught Tristian on the jaw. "Geeze, Kikyo it's just me . . . are you ok?" Tristian began apologetic, he was rubbing his jaw but then concern clouded over his eyes. I wondered how long I had been in a daze over Angel Xavier. I shuddered as I tried to put Angel Xavier out of my mind. Thankfully, I was staring down at my open *Ibsen* book, and so it looked like I was concentrating on that, instead of my thoughts being a million miles away on Angel Xavier. "Oh I'm so sorry, did I hurt you? Amor, dinner should be just about ready, you wanna set the table?" I quickly found my voice, and was rubbing my fist as I went to get dinner. I was stiff from sitting so long in reverie and not moving, but I didn't let on. I couldn't understand why I was so obsessed about Angel Xavier, was it his mannerisms, his voice, his violet eyes, or a combination of all three? I had to stop, Tristian was saying something, but once again, my mind had drifted. "I'm sorry, Tristian, what were you saying?" I asked hoping to disguise my quavering voice.

"I was just asking if you had a good day Hun, you looked dumbfounded when you were walking to your locker at the end of the day was everything ok?" I could feel myself flush at the mere thought of Angel Xavier, and his attitude when he saw me with Tristian, sent my flush deeper. I couldn't find the words I needed, and Tristian was waiting for a response. I had to mentally shake myself into coherency before I could speak. "Um . . . well, I don't know what his problem was, maybe he thought he had a chance with me or something, I don't know." It was a feeble response, but the best I could muster at the moment. Tristian took the roast from me and began to fill his plate, as I went about filling our glasses with iced tea. I saw the un-placated look in Tristian's face at my words, and felt I had to make the atmosphere around us better. "Sorry, Tristian . . ." I apologized looking deep into his gorgeous chocolate brown eyes, "I don't know, but something about Angel Xavier, is *intriguing* almost like he has a secret I'm in on but don't remember or understand, it's weird. Anyway, the odd thing about him is that, in every class, he spoke only to me. You know, whenever someone is new, or back in his case, they usually talk to as many people as they can, and all the other classmates want to know about the new person, but no one took much notice of him, and today, people more to me than to him, like I said . . . weird."

"So, what is this, Angel Xavier like?" Tristian had an odd tone to his voice that I was unfamiliar with, his face was flushed and his eyes were dark. "Well to tell you the truth . . ." I stammered, "all, I know is that his parents are divorced, he lives with his dad, whose a stock broker, and his mom is a teacher with autistic children, out in the suburbs somewhere. He say's he likes living with his dad, because since he's always so busy, Angel is pretty much left alone, and he likes it that way. But really that's all I know." I left out all the features of his face that I had memorized over the course of the day. "Oh, and also Mrs. Mertleman has us working on an **Ibsen** paper for our final." I added, just so that he knew, that I would be working with Angel Xavier. "Did you know him before he transferred back?" I asked not really knowing how to feel either way if Tristian had or had not known him. "Yeah, I knew him, but not well, I think we may have had a class or two freshman year, but . . . well, ok then." Was all Tristian said. I could tell his mood was still different, but I let it go, was he jealous I wondered?

After dinner, Tristian helped me clean up, and we watched a half hour sitcom, on TV, before Tristian said he had to go. He was still in his sulking mood, and I really didn't know what to do to make it better. Barely a word was spoken between us before Tristian said good bye. When I had walked Tristian to the garage, he said he'd call me when he got home, and that he'd see me tomorrow. All I could do was nod my head and walk slowly back to the house. I was feeling low, but the thoughts of Angel Xavier invaded my mind, and left me frustrated and anxious.

It was still early, and I did have laundry to do, so I went about stripping my bed, and emptying the hamper. I tossed everything down the stairs, not from the terror that I usually felt but more from convenience. When I was down in the basement, I still felt the usual trepidations, but they were dulled somehow. As if by facing the dark shadows of the past, I was able to go about my business without the horror of the unknown lurking in every corner. Since I was already in the basement, I picked up a broom, and commenced to sweep up the inevitable dust, and cobwebs. I fell into another wave of deep concentration over the events of the day, when the ringing phone jerked me out of my trance. I ran to the laundry room, where I had left the cordless phone, and was a bit breathless as I answered on the third ring. "Hello, querido, are you home now?" I asked still somewhat winded. "Yeah, I'm home . . ." Tristian said in an odd way, maybe he was still moody from our evening. "look, I wanna apologize, I know that I acted like a jerk today, Kikyo, it's just that well first seeing this guy's reaction to me, threw me off, and then with you saying he was intriguing, well anyway, for what it's worth I'm sorry." "Oh, Tristian, I'm the one who's sorry, it's just that this is all new to me, you know that I love you, and that will never change. It's because of you that I can even notice anyone at all. Please honey don't waste another minute stressing about Angel Xavier." But even as I said those words, I felt like I was hiding or holding something back, I didn't fully understand what was going on within me, but for Tristian's sake, I had better get my head clear, and my priorities straight.

"Hey Kikyo, what were you doing that you sounded breathless?" Tristian asked, back to his usual light tone. "Oh . . . wow . . . let me tell you where I am, where I've been since you left really . . ." I had pushed Angel Xavier to the back of my mind and concentrated only on Tristian. "I had to do laundry, and since I was already down here I was sweeping up the dust and cobwebs. Honey, I've been down here the whole time, and I can handle it now, I'm still jumpy, but I'm not a wreck like I was before. Thank you, if it weren't for all your help, I'd probably still be shivering of freight with all the lights on." And even as I said it, I realized that this was true. If not for Tristian, who knows that Angel Xavier would even have been compelled to speak to me, he would probably regret having come to my school. "Darling, I love you, I'll pick you up tomorrow, I gotta go. Sleep well." I said my good night's too and clicked off the phone, and put the wet clothes in the drier, turned off the lights and headed back upstairs, to ready myself for bed.

I immediately began to worry about Tristian when the phone rang, about ten o'clock, I wasn't expecting Tristian to call me again tonight, so I figured something must've been wrong. "Amor, are you ok, is something wrong?" I asked with rising panic in my voice. "Well thanks for the endearment, but no this is not . . . Tristian, its Angel, how are you Kikyo?" his voice oozed with smoothness, and I had to literally shake my head in order to clear it. "Angel . . . ?" I was totally perplexed by his call "Um . . . how did you get my number . . . sorry I don't mean to be rude, but um . . . what do you want?" my words came out harsher than I wanted, but it was just a reflex to the unexpectedness of his casual tone, and the fact that I wondered how he did in fact have my number. "Oh, I'm sorry, did I bother you? Were you asleep already?" his voice was liquid silk as the words, melted from the phone and into my ready ear. "Um . . . no . . . no bother, I was just getting ready for bed, what was on your mind?" I tried to sound as casual as he did, but I'm sure that I was way off.

"Well, I just wanted to thank you for being so nice to me on my first day back. I hope I wasn't too abusive of your time." The way Angel's words, seeped into my soul made it hard to argue with him. "Oh . . . not at all . . . don't worry about it." I had to force myself to concentrate and not sound like an awestruck idiot. "Well, look Kikyo, I actually wanted to know if you weren't seeing anyone seriously, because I wanted to ask you out sometime." His words, filled with total confidence took me off guard, and I momentarily forgot that Tristian even existed. "Um . . . Sorry, Angel, but I have a boyfriend, but we can still be friends, I hope you understand." I was surprised by my own words, would Tristian even feel threatened for me to be friends with Angel Xavier I wondered. "Oh, well too bad for me, but hey at least we can be friends as you said. So anyway, did you start reading Ibsen yet?" our conversation went on for about half an hour longer, without anymore mention of dating. I had never had a conversation like this before, since I didn't have any girlfriends, and Tristian was only recently in my life, I was feeling exhilarated. It was good to talk to someone other than Tristian, not that talking to him was boring; it was just that Angel was new, exciting, and had a different perspective. Angel Xavier didn't know my past, my most recent present, or even my deepest darkest secrets like Tristian did. I could tell Tristian anything, no matter how crazy or embarrassing, and know that Tristian would not ever judge me; he would just love me all the more.

Angel and I said our good-night's and hung up. I drifted in and out of sleep, and was restless as I tried to calm my swimming brain. It was like watching a tennis game in my head between Tristian and Angel Xavier. I was weighing the similarities and differences between the two. I don't recall exactly when I finally slept and dreamed, but it was disturbing, and I woke up with the alarm buzzing in my ear. The dream was a foggy in my memory and I tried to push it to the back of my brain. All I could remember about the dream as I was getting ready for school; was that Tristian and Angel Xavier were having a standoff, and I was in the middle a hand on each of their chests, keeping them at arms length away from each other before they tore into one another. I ran through the house like a madwoman getting ready and swallowing down some cereal and toast, and put out a pack of chicken to thaw in the bottom shelf of the refrigerator. I pulled a brush through my hair and ran out the door, as Tristian was just pulling up to my house. He quickly got out, and held the car door open for me, as I locked my house up for the day.

Tristian greeted me with an apologetic half-smile, and open arms. I gratefully let him wrap his strong arms around me and let all the tensions in me melt away. He kissed, my head, my cheeks, my eyelids, and stopped himself before he could kiss my lips, and send me to my predictable ridged response. He hugged me tighter one last time before letting me go, and closing the car door behind me. When Tristian was behind the wheel, and the car was moving, he took my hand like he usually did, and entwined his fingers with mine. He turned to me again with that apologetic half-smile, but before he could apologize once again about his reaction yesterday, I stopped him. "Tristian, please no harm was done, let's forget about it ok, besides, I want us to be always content, and I don't like to see you upset. I love you, and you are my life, my reason for being who I am today. So please no more apologies. There is nothing to feel bad about." I squeezed his hand in mine, and if not for the seatbelt, tethering me to my seat, I would've kissed his cheek, but I settled for the back of his hand, and his fingertips instead. He nodded in compliance and said he loved me as well.

"Kikyo, I've got practice again today, so I want you to take the car home again, and one of the guys will drop me off again later ok?" he said this after we had parked and he was already handing me the keys. "Well, querido, why don't you invite your friend for dinner, I'd really like to meet some of your friends. I know that I've taken up so much of your time away from them, I'm eternally grateful and I'd like to re-pay your friends for not giving you such a hard time about it, what do you think?" I hadn't planned to say it, but the words were out before I could rein them back in. I was still unsure as I saw him weighing it over in his mind. Thankfully, Tristian flashed my favorite smile at me and said he'd ask a couple of the guys if they'd like to meet me and stay for dinner. "I'll let you know how many will join us for dinner after school." He hugged me again, and began to turn away towards school, before pausing and turning back to me once again. "Thank you Kikyo, I really appreciate this, but are you sure your ready for so many strangers?" the compassion was back in his eyes, and it nearly tore my heart in two, I swallowed the lump that had formed in my throat, and smiled back at him, "Absolutely, if I can sleep nightmare free and tolerate the basement, then, I think I'm ready." He nodded, and walked away, as did I.

Chapter Six

Competition

I floated off to my locker, to collect my morning books, and get to home room. Angel Xavier was casually leaning against my locker, his books already cradled in his arms, waiting for me. He had a huge grin on his face; that cut his dimples even deeper into his cheeks. I could see the brilliant pearl white of his perfect teeth, and his full ruby red lips. From the distance, I was able to focus my attention on the rest of him, not just his exquisite face. Angel Xavier was just slightly taller than my Tristian, about by an inch or so, his build was more muscular and broader shouldered than Tristian. His hair also long was wavy and the lightest brown almost a blond, he wore it loose so that it curled over and below his shoulders. Angel Xavier, wore a thin light blue, form fitting long sleeved sweater that he had pushed up to his elbows and his khakis were perfectly pressed, even his soft soled loafers, looked like they had been recently polished. Angel Xavier, looked nothing like any of the boys that attended this school, most boys wore jeans, tee shirts and sneakers. Angel Xavier's attire even rivaled that of Tristian, or any of the male teachers. I was awestruck as I took all this in and kept my emotions in check before I could ferociously blush, and embarrass myself.

"Good morning Kikyo" Angel said when I had drawn close enough. He had a secret smile on the corners of his mouth like he knew what I was thinking and I had to avert my eyes. "Good morning Angel, how are you today?" He had stepped aside so that I could open my locker, as he continued with some more pleasantries. Standing this close to Angel, I could smell his personal fragrance; it was a scent much more potent than that of Tristian that I had to bury my face deep within my locker while I regained my composure. I wondered idly how I was going to get through the day without making a fool of myself in front of Angel Xavier. "Are you coming out of there anytime soon Kikyo?" Angel kidded me, and I quickly shut the locker and followed him into homeroom. We took our seats, and I noticed that all the girls were staring at Angel Xavier, and the boys were all staring at me, but before I could say anything or even turn away, Mr. Kotwazinski walked into the room and called the class to order. Angel Xavier had been oblivious to the fact that the entire class stared at us when we had entered.

Mr. Kotwazinski, took attendance and was giving the daily announcements, as he walked up and down the aisles, passing around the ballots for Prom Queen and King, normally I would have not paid it any mind, but what caught my attention was not the fact that Tristian was up for King, that was to be expected, but that I was up for queen! The horror, who could have done this to me? "And so lets all congratulate our very own Kikyo, who is up for queen . . ." cheers erupted and Angel was up with the rest of the class clapping and whistling as I turned all shades of red.

When the bell rang for us to get to our next class, Angel Xavier reached over and touched my arm once again. It was like when you touch metal and get a shock, except his hand was cold, like he had been holding a block of ice during class. "Congratulations, you got my vote Your Highness." I was blushing as I tried to avoid all the eyes that were on me, while I made my way out of home room. I was headed towards Math, when I was stopped by a group of girls whom I had some classes with, they were congratulating me and saying they hoped I would win. I thanked them and again wondered if it was some kind of mistake or worse a cruel joke. I received the same reception when I walked into my math class. Mrs. Browning had to call the class to order so that we can begin. I tried desperately to hide in my corner and bury my face in my book, but everyone still continued to smile at me and give me thumbs up when Mrs. Browning had her back turned. I felt like I would die.

When math was over, I was afraid to face English, and hear what Angel Xavier would have to say further about my nomination. Oh why couldn't the earth just open up and swallow me alive? Angel was waiting for me, by our desks with a huge grin and surrounded by about half the class, all asking him about himself, and vying for his friendship. When I came closer, Angel waved away his entourage and had eyes and ears only for me. Mrs. Mertleman congratulated me and began class. I tried hard to concentrate on the lesson of the day, but I couldn't focus on anything Mrs. Mertleman was saying. All of a sudden, I had a deep dull itch that couldn't and wouldn't be scratched over my sweater. I had to ask to be excused, so that I could try to take care of the problem in private. But before I could voice my need, Angel Xavier asked to be excused, he said he had suddenly come down with a headache, and needed to see the nurse. Mrs. Mertleman asked if I could show Angel Xavier the way.

I was confused by the way this had worked out. It was as if Angel Xavier knew that I needed to get out of class, and he had used his excuse to do it. I rose from my seat and Angel Xavier followed me out the door. The class was already half over and I knew that Mrs. Mertleman didn't expect us back. When we were out in the hallway, with our hall passes in hand, I asked Angel Xavier if he was really feeling bad, he looked like he did, but I didn't really believe it. He turned to me, when we were away from the class with the door closed behind us. "I feel fine, but you looked like you needed to get out of there, was I right?" he asked with his violet eyes boring into mine. When I looked deep in his eyes, I forgot myself, and anything around me. I had to stammer, just to speak. "Um . . . yeah, I really did need to get out, but now I feel fine." It was weird, I was feeling so itchy, and suddenly the urgency to scratch was gone. But we couldn't stay in the hallway. Angel Xavier was looking at me, like he had some secret, and the corners of his exquisite ruby red mouth held a smile. "Come on, I know where we can go hide-out." He grabbed my hand, and I barely noticed the icy coldness of his stone hard grip on my hand. He pulled me along behind him, and led me towards the auditorium balcony. "No one will find us here" he said as he pried open one of the side doors, and we slipped into the silent darkness, of the balcony.

I should've been alarmed by the way that his skin seemed to glow, in the darkness. The faint lights from the stage barely reached us, but somehow Angel Xavier was illuminated as if from within his own skin. His violet eyes still held mine, and it seemed as if he could read my thoughts or deeper even, my soul. I felt dizzy and numb at the same time, as my mind was racing with endless questions that my mouth could not voice, or even keep up with. I wanted to ask him, how he knew I needed to get out of class, I wanted to ask him, why he had befriended only me, and I wanted ask him, how it had come to be that he seemed so sure of me, when even I wasn't sure of me. But the latter question made no sense, yet somehow made complete sense. But I kept my questions and concerns to myself, as I was still mute, and staring dumbly at his perfect features.

I felt as if he knew all my questions, and wordlessly put the answers into my mind. When he finally spoke, his voice was like a whisper that caressed my senses. I was swooning, just from the close proximity to him. His scent was sending my olfactory senses into overdrive, and I felt compelled to reach out and touch my fingertips to his ruby lips. They were just as cold and hard as his hand, and for some odd reason, I had no reaction to this. I was still dazed and beginning to lean in closer to him, when the stupor I was under, was suddenly broken by the shrill bell marking the end of second period. Realization finally began to creep back to me, and

I jumped up and out of my seat, headed for the balcony door. Without a word, I bolted from the darkness, and left Angel Xavier behind me.

The events in the auditorium played over and over in my head during Biology. I couldn't believe that we had actually sat in the darkness for half a period, not verbally speaking. I bet he thought I was some kind of dumb freak from the way I stared at him wordlessly, and annoyingly foolishly. I didn't know how I was going to avoid Angel Xavier for the rest of the day. I was feeling like such an idiot. What had come over me, I wondered. It wasn't in my nature to act like such a fool. My mind kept going back to the way Angel Xavier, looked into my eyes, the way he felt, and the way that I left, so abruptly and rudely.

Lunch was next and I just knew that he would be waiting for me after class, to walk me to my locker then to lunch. I was actually feeling sick, as the thousands of butterflies in my stomach, flew around in a million different directions. What had I done? The guilt of my actions was weighing heavily on me, as the eternal seconds hung in mid-air, and refused to tic by. This was by far the slowest passing hour of my life. It was as if time had stopped, or slowed down enough to drive me mad. If I could get through the rest of the day without running into Angel Xavier, I think I would be all right, but if luck just happened to intervene before I could escape to the ladies room, then I wouldn't know what to say to Angel Xavier.

I knew that I wanted to avoid seeing him, I was so confused by my own reaction to him, that I didn't really think I could face Angel Xavier anymore today, but at the same time, something compelled me to want to be near him, to reach out and touch him once again, and to feel his penetrating gaze on me. I had a million questions for him, questions that I needed to voice. I was so confused by him, that I didn't actually know what questions to ask. Around Angel Xavier, I felt normal, I felt complete, not like with Tristian, this was a whole different level for me. Around Angel Xavier, I felt despite the fact that I was so dazed by him, I felt powerful somehow, like if the confidence he exuded was passed on to me somehow. It was exhilarating to just be in his company. But what on earth was compelling me to feel like this? I had only just met this strange new boy, and knew nothing about him really; could it have been the fact that he was someone who didn't know me? But I so wanted him to know me, to know the real me, the "me" that only Tristian knew. But then this dilemma brought me back to Tristian, my beloved Tristian, who brought me back from the brink of my own personal insanity. My Tristian, who knew all there was to know about me. My Tristian who didn't judge me, only loved me more with each passing day.

I was startled back to reality, and out of my own musings by the bell, tolling out the end of class, and the start of my lunch period. It was time to face Angel Xavier. My heart sank down to my feet, when he was nowhere in sight. Avoidance was my goal, and I had achieved it. I was all the more confused by my feelings, but never the less I made a bee-line for the ladies room. I quickly locked the stall door behind me, and let the cold tile wall, ease some of the tension from my body as I slid to the floor with my knees pulled up under my chin. I tried my best to sort out all the conflicting feelings between Tristian and Angel Xavier. The butterflies were back in my stomach, flying a mile a minute and threatening to bring up my breakfast. I had to lower my head between my knees just to keep from swooning, and count backwards from a hundred to calm my nerves.

I couldn't explain why I was having such strong unnatural feelings towards Angel Xavier, it was Tristian whom I loved, but then why was I feeling like I was betraying Angel Xavier, by forcing my thoughts to Tristian, when it should have been the other way around? My head was spinning and I was grateful I was already on the floor, I could feel the bile begin to rise in my throat, and clung to the commode, just in the nick of time. Never had I had such a violent physical reaction to any situation I was in. I was all the more confused, but had to pull myself together, before it was time to leave. If I decided to leave now and go home, what would I tell Tristian? How could I possibly explain my current state of mind to him? I had to chastise myself, and regain my composure, no need to worry Tristian, he was bringing some friends over tonight and I couldn't afford to let him down.

I was glad that I always carried a bottle of water and mints in my bag. I rinsed my mouth out, and sucked on a couple of mints. I was feeling better, and needed to decide what my next step would be. Should I go home and leave Tristian a note taped to my locker, or suck it up and finish the day? I knew that I wouldn't see Angel Xavier, in anymore classes today, and if I played my cards right, I could possibly avoid him at the end of the day also if I lagged behind in my Spanish class, I knew Tristian would wait for me by my locker, but I felt that with Tristian around, Angel would not wait around for me. This was the best case scenario I could hope for, and not lead my Tristian to any unnecessary worries or suspicions.

I was grateful for the fact that I had the ladies room all to myself, and no one knew about my "episode". I was able to put on my mask of contentment and walk out as the bell rang, without anyone being any the wiser. I headed for gym, and the chance to blow off some of my built-up energy in a game of dodge ball. It seemed we would be playing this for at least the rest of the week, and I was secretly glad for it. It was beginning to feel like I was going to need an outlet for the unusual range of emotions that had suddenly formed in me. P.E. was good, as I showered, I thought about what tonight would be like, it was something new to me, and I wasn't used to letting anyone into my private world. I had to wonder to myself about what would Tristian's friends think of me. Would I even know any of them? I'm sure that I had to have some classes with someone who knew Tristian, but since I had been so oblivious to the world around me, would I even recognize anyone? I put the thought out of my mind, as I raced to dress and get on to my last class of the day.

As I raced through the hallway to get to my class on time, I scanned the halls for Angel Xavier, but not seeing him anywhere, I was left saddened yet again. Once in my seat, I mindlessly doodled in my notebook, and stared out the window. Mr. Kotwazinski had to call on me a couple of times, in order for me to come back to earth, from my space-out. I was able to answer his questions, and go back to staring out the window. When class was over I was determined to lag behind, but found myself rushing for the door instead. Once again I scoured the halls for any sign of Angel Xavier, but again to my disappointment, I didn't see him. I was dejected and anxious as I headed to my locker. As soon as I saw Tristian coming towards me, all the joy that he seemed to exude, seemed to be contagious, as I too matched his happiness. He swept me up in his arms, as I blushed profusely and he kissed the top of my head.

"Ahh, Kikyo, querida, it's been such a long day. I've missed you from the moment that we parted this morning. Did you have a good day?" I was like a prisoner between my locker and Tristian's arm giving no hope of escape. But this prison suited me just fine. I didn't want to worry him with the events of my day, I figured I'd just keep that to myself, there was plenty of time for me to muse over all that had happened to me later, in the privacy of my home. "I've missed you as well Tristian. So, how many guests will we have tonight?" I needed to get my mind on a different track, and really did need to know, so that I can prepare dinner. "Oh, yeah, right, um I talked to the guys, and we're having three more for dinner tonight,

I hope that's ok." Tristian looked like he was ready to burst at the seams from his giddy joy, and I just wanted to be just as excited, but Angel Xavier kept circling around my thoughts. "Oh yeah, I just wanted to know, so that I can plan accordingly. I do hope that they are comfortable. Anyway, I'll make something special. Now, I gotta go. I love you Tristian." I had to stretch up on my tiptoes, so that I could kiss his cheek. He dropped his keys into my waiting hand, and kissed both my cheeks, before clutching me in a bear hug. "See you around six, amor." He called out as he headed towards his practice.

I collected the necessary books, I needed for homework, and pretty much floated off to the school parking lot. The day's events had been filed away into a corner of my mind for later revision and obsessing. I wasn't paying much attention to where I was going, and tripped over my own two feet, sending my books flying all around me. I was more embarrassed than hurt, and a little startled that a girl (whose name escaped me) I had English with, stooped down to help me pick up my mess. "Are you ok, Kikyo?" my cheeks were blazing due to my public clumsiness, and I flashed a weak smile at her. "Yeah, I'm fine thanks . . . . sorry, what's your name?" with a sweet giggle, she held out my books for me to take. "I'm Amber; it's nice to "officially" meet you Kikyo. She held out her hand, and I shook it. "Walk you to your car?" Amber was already in step with me and headed towards Tristian's car. We walked the short distance to the car and again I thanked Amber for her help and kindness. She was parked a few cars down and waved at me with a smile. See you tomorrow Kikyo, have a good night." "Thanks again Amber, you too." I waved back and got in the car, my embarrassing spill already forgotten, I headed home.

As I drove home, I turned up the radio which Tristian always kept either turned way low or totally off. I replayed the events of the day in my head, and didn't even realize that I was driving subconsciously until I was turning into the ally behind my house. I locked the garage behind me and headed towards the back kitchen door, when something caught me eye, under the porch where I kept the lawnmower, snow blower and yard supplies. I let it go, and went up the stairs to my back door. I set my bag down, hung my coat on the back of a kitchen chair, and headed to the bathroom to find an elastic band to pick up my hair.

I hadn't reopened any old scars or added new ones in a few nights, so my scars were beginning to heal and fade. I was going to have to inspect the rest of my scars later, but for now, I had to get dinner started. I set about making a meatloaf with mashed potatoes and gravy. While the oven did its work, I made a salad, and sliced some bread to complete our meal. I checked the time on the microwave and went to change before Tristian and his friends arrived. I was running a brush through my hair when I heard Tristian calling from the living room. "Be right out" I called from the bathroom. I took one more look at myself, took a deep breath and steadied myself for whatever this night may bring.

"Guys, this is my Kikyo, Kikyo, theses are my friends, Auggie, Victor, Chris, Omar and Edgar." "Nice to meet you all" I said as I shook each hand that was offered to me. "I do hope you guys are all hungry, there is plenty of food, and your all welcome to it, the bathroom is right through the hall third door on your right, if you guys wanna wash up before dinner, Tristian can you help me set the table please?"

I recognized most of the boys from my various classes over the course of the years, and even one from grade school. I knew that this was a huge step towards a new chapter in my life, and Tristian did his best to put me at ease. Once we were alone in the kitchen, Tristian pulled me to him, in a tight embrace, and held me so comfortably close; I didn't want him to let me go. "It's gonna be fine Kikyo, trust me, your gonna be fine, they're gonna love you." We finished setting the table and met some of the boys in the living room, while the rest finished washing up. I was a little nervous as the shyness in me refused to be stifled, but the guys were nice, and didn't ask me many questions that required more than a yes or no answer. When the rest of the group joined us, I led everyone to the dining room, "Guy's dinner is served."

Dinner was nice; everyone talked at once wanting to know about me, and my past. No one was rude, pushy or pressed for any answers. I was surprised at how easily the conversation flowed from me, it was like if I had known the boys forever, and I was relaxed and comfortable, by the time dinner and the night came to an end. We had school tomorrow and everyone had to get home. The boy's that had girlfriends promised to introduce us, and said we'd all be good friends. One of the guy's I think it was Edgar, suggested we all go to the movies or something Saturday, if the girlfriends were game. We said our goodbye's and waved them away after walking them to the one car they had all came in, good thing it was a van, because it was a car full.

After the guy's drove away, Tristian and I went back inside, and cleaned up the dishes and leftovers. After we were done, Tristian once again pulled me close to him, "Kikyo, amor I love you, you were just as awesome as I said you would be, the guy's all liked you, and I promise you, the clouds of your past will no longer linger as long as I'm around to chase them away." He held my face up to his, and gently leaned in to kiss me, when the memory of Angel Xavier burned like molten lava behind my lids, and I pulled away. "S-s-sorry, I can't, Tristian, please forgive me." I broke free from his embrace, and turned to face away from him. "Hey, it's ok, I'm the one who should be sorry, Kikyo, I know you're not ready for that kind of intimacy, please, I won't do that again, until your ready, now come here." He wiped the tears from my eyes, and held me close again. This boy was a saint, and I let my tears of shame flow, as he held me to him, and my heart slowed to beat in sync with his. Why couldn't I bring myself to break free from that emotional barricade that held me at bay? Why was it so easy to do so with Angel Xavier? I had to ponder those questions later when I was alone with my assaulting thoughts. For now, I had to make it up to Tristian, I knew I hurt him when I pulled away, but I didn't know how to make it better.

It was late, and I knew Tristian had to go. He kept insisting that my reaction was normal and that he didn't blame me or think less of me, but I was certain that my rejection no matter how involuntary it was had cut him like a knife. He told me to quit apologizing and to just let time get me to the point where I can be ok with the intimacy that our first kiss would bring. We said our good nights and I waved to him form the open garage door, as he promised to be here for me in the morning. My head was swimming with confusion as I locked up the garage, and headed back towards the back door.

I saw a flash of light glint off of something once again from under the porch, and went to investigate what it had been that had caught my eye earlier today.

I had to stoop down to see where the object of my attention was coming from. It was wedged between the blades of the seldom used rake, caked in long ago dried mud, it was just a bottle cap, and nothing more, but just the uncertainty of what it was had sent my heart beating against my chest, and a cold sweat had covered me in a thin film. I shook off the all-too familiar feeling of being watched and quickly went back up into the safety of my house. The phone was ringing as I entered through the kitchen, and I caught it, I think on the fourth ring. "Hey, sorry querido, I was outside for a minute, did you ring long, are you almost home?" my words ran together so fast I was out of breath, but the voice on the line, knocked what was left in me right out. "Whoa, whoa, whoa, Kikyo, get a grip, this is Angel." "Oh, sorry Angel, um, can you call me back in like fifteen minutes or so, I don't have call waiting and Tristian is probably trying to get through, sorry." "Yeah sure, no problem, you sure it wont be too late to call?" "Um, no not at all, talk to you soon, bye." I hung up the phone with shaking hands, and was about to pick it up to dial Tristian, when the phone rang, and startled me. "Hello, Tristian I was just about to dial you, sorry amor, but I was checking something outside and missed your call." "Kikyo, I swear if you wouldn't have answered I would've turned around and came right back, I know I'm being a little obsessive and overprotective of you, but honestly amor, if something more were to happen to you, I don't know what I would do." "Tristian, I really am sorry about it honey, but I do understand your point. I love you for loving me so deeply, I can never repay you for all you do for me, but trust that you are truly appreciated and extremely loved for it." "Kikyo, you are the vain of my existence, and without you, I would chose not to exist at all." "Tristian, you speak like I'm going somewhere, trust me when I say, I'm here with you for the long haul, you can't get rid of me so easily." "Babe, I'm home now, but I'll see you tomorrow, and we'll continue this. Sleep well my love; I'll be by to pick you up in the morning. I love you Kikyo" "As do I Tristian, sleep well."

By the end of our conversation, I had temporarily forgotten about Angel and my uneasiness before finding the bottle cap. I had some homework to do, but before I settled down to do it, I went to change and get comfortable. I was just pulling up my hair, when the phone rang once again. "Hello, Kikyo, can you talk now?" "Um, Hi Angel, yeah, um how are you?" "Well Kikyo, I just wanted to know how you were doing, after . . . what happened today, you ran out of the balcony so fast I didn't get a chance to talk to you, and my third period class rang long, so when I didn't catch you after Biology, I waited for you at our lunch table, but you never showed, I figured you needed time to sort things out." The memory of my hiding out in the ladies room came crashing back to me, and I blushed with the embarrassment of the feelings Angel Xavier stirred in me and of getting sick from the butterfly frenzy in my stomach. I still didn't know what to say to Angel about it or how I would face him at school tomorrow.

"Angel, about today, I think I need to apologize to you, I'm sorry about my actions today, I don't want to give you the wrong impression of me, and I don't want to lead you on, but I'm with Tristian, and I can't hurt him, by what I've done. Trust me, if I could rewind the day and redo it, I would." "Kikyo, I understand all you're saying, it was just a moment of weakness, I know you're with Tristian, and even though I wish it weren't so, I do need to respect that. Kikyo, I do hope that this little "incident" doesn't come between our friendship, because it means a lot to me." "No, no, not at all Angel, in fact if we can pretend that it didn't happen at all, I would greatly appreciate it, I'm not asking you lie for me, because even I won't do that to Tristian, but I will ask as a friend that this stays between us." "Don't you worry your pretty little head about it one bit Kikyo, like I said I totally understand where you're coming from, but I also want you to know that if it were to end with Tristian, I will always be standing by in the wings." "Angel, I don't want you to give up anything for me, trust me, I'm not good for you and I wouldn't feel right to know your just waiting for me and Tristian to end. So please, please, please understand that today was a mistake and I don't want to lose your friendship, but if I know your waiting around for me, then I'm afraid that I can't allow that and would need to break off our friendship, no matter who it hurts more." "Kikyo, don't trip, I got you, and you needn't worry about a thing, "nothing" happened, and were cool ok?" "Ok, Angel, thanks for calling me, I really did need to get this straightened out. See you tomorrow?" "See you in home room, oh and Kikyo, sleep well."

The line cut off before I could react to the same phrase that Tristian had used. I didn't know why, but my head was so confused by Angel's feeling's for me, that I knew homework was going to be impossible to concentrate on, thankfully, none of it was due until the end of the week. I needed to come to terms that the way I felt for Angel was not beneficial to any of us, no good could come of me letting the feelings I have for Angel surface again. I had to vow to myself that Angel, no matter how magnetic he was to me, no matter how electrifying he was to me, and no matter how devastatingly right I felt with him, I would not under any circumstances betray my Tristian again. Tristian was the reason, I even noticed Angel in the first place, if it weren't for Tristian, I probably would have graduated as the same zombie, I had embodied throughout all of high school. No. I owed Tristian more than just my gratefulness and loyalty; I owed this savior my life. True, I was the one who called him, and sought him out, but he answered my call and accepted my plea and saved me from my dark abyss. No. My Tristian deserves more than I can ever give him, he saved me from myself, and that was a huge feat in itself.

Tristian, was now my reason for existence, my reason to not fade to black once again, my reason, to face my past, and once and for all, break free from the prison, I had created for myself. The very prison that I thought was to protect everyone from me, as I suffered in solitary silence. My self-imposed exile into my own confused and clouded mind was now at an end. I went about getting ready for bed, in a daze. I put out my clothes for tomorrow, put my books back in my bag, and went to brush my teeth. I was dreading seeing Angel in the morning but at the same time longed for it. I was going to need to bury those feelings deep down, and keep them there.

I curled up under my blankets, and tried to recall all the details of the dinner, and all I had learned of Tristian's friends, but it was useless, every time I tried to concentrate on a specific moment, my mind wandered back to the dark balcony, and the way time seemed to be suspended when Angel looked deep within me. It was like Angel had plucked my very thoughts from my mind, and knew what I was thinking, and all I wanted to ask him. Angel's deep violet eyes, had bore into mine and it felt as if he had silently extracted every memory, thought, action, and revelation that I had ever had. I needn't ever explain myself to him, because it was as if, he knew me better than Tristian knew me, or even far better than even I knew me. Angel Xavier was a strange, complex and utterly mesmerizing person. I didn't know how, but I had to find a way, to decipher all the mysteries that made-up my new friend. The fact that he seemed to emit light from within, or that he cooled the air around him, or even that when I touched his ruby red lips, they were hard as real ruby's meant nothing to me. All that mattered was that he quickened my heart and stopped my breath. Angel Xavier didn't need to touch me, for me to feel the electrical currents that seemed to flow from him to me. I shook with the memory of the precious stolen moments we had shared in the darkened balcony, and with Angel's name on my lips and his face behind my eyelids, I faded off to sleep.

Chapter Seven

Confrontation

I awoke to the sound of a deafening shrieking, and it took me a few seconds to realize that it was once again coming from me. It had been weeks since my nightmares had played a staring roll in my dreams. Something had changed in my dreams. I was once again being followed, but this time it felt more familiar, not in the sense that I was reliving a prior dream, but in the sense that my pursuer was someone I knew.

This couldn't possibly be happening again, I thought I had put it all past me now, that somehow my basement revelations, and Tristian's unwavering support had put an end to all the nightmares. I reached for the phone to call Tristian, but reconsidered when I saw not surprisingly that it was once again 3:00 am. I hugged myself tightly, and curled into a fetal position, as the waves of the final vestiges of my dream faded away.

The dream had been familiar but different. I was under the porch, digging for the object of my earlier attention. I walked as if in slow motion; to the rake that held what I already knew was a bottle cap entombed in the dried mud, except that upon closer inspection, it wasn't a bottle cap, it was the very ring that I had found under the shelving unit in the basement tool room. I had totally forgotten about that ring, at the moment, I didn't even know what I had done with it, I wondered if it held some kind of clue, or if it was just a coincidence. I pushed that thought from my mind, and tried my best to go back to sleep.

Sleep refused to come to me, and I was grateful for the homework that I couldn't concentrate on before to occupy my time. It was creeping on three thirty when I finally unfolded myself from my bed, and made my way to the kitchen for a cup of coffee. The nightmare had upset me, but nothing quite like they had done before, I checked myself for new scratches, but found none. I splashed cold water on my face to chase away the sleepiness that still clung to me, and retrieved my long abandoned i-pod from my bag.

With the buds in my ears, and my homework laid out in front of me, I did more work than I had originally set out to do. I surprised myself that I was able to get so much done, in a short amount of time, or could it have been that since now for the first time, I was actually aware of what I was doing instead of in my former zombie-like state? Either way, I was pleased with my progress, not only in my academics, but in my life as well.

Tristian was my own personal safety net and cheerleader all in one. Then there was Angel Xavier, he summoned feelings in me that I never knew I possessed. Tristian held my heart, my love, and my eternal gratitude, but Angel Xavier, he held my soul, and my every emotion. How long could I continue to deny my feelings for Angel Xavier? Angel had awakened something in me that I couldn't understand or comprehend, but every time, I thought of Angel, I felt that I was betraying Tristian. Tristian was my beloved, my savior, my reason for existence. I needed to put an end to my irrational feelings and longings for Angel Xavier, before I hurt Tristian.

I was willing to endure the pain that I knew would inevitably come with not letting Angel's strong-hold on me continue, if it meant that Tristian would be non-the-wiser of my uncharacteristic behavior towards and around Angel Xavier. Maybe I was going to have to let Angel know that as far as our common classes went, there was nothing I could do about them, but going forward, waiting for me after classes and lunch would have to stop. The plan seemed like it was the right thing to do, but my very core cried out in need of Angel's presence. It was like if, Tristian was the lifesaver I clung to, but Angel was the deserted island I swam to.

I was deep in my debate between the two men in my life, when the alarm clock rang from my bedroom, and buzzed me back to reality. I had to rush to get ready for school, and was done in the nick of time. As soon as I stepped out of the house, Tristian was halfway up the stairs to ring the bell. "Sorry, querido, I was running a little late." I gave him a weak smile, and let him embrace me. "Kikyo, are you ok, you look tired?" "Yeah, I'm fine, it was just a long day yesterday, I had some homework I needed to get done, but I'm good." "Ok, if you're sure." Tristian held the car door open for me, and came around, to drive us off to another day of school.

As we drove off, Tristian took my hand like always, and talked non-stop about last night's dinner. His friends really liked me and wondered why I had gone from dark clouds to sunny skies practically overnight. Tristian refused to believe that it was all because of him, that it had something to do with "time healing all wounds". I suppose there was some truth to that also, but for the most part, my awakening came from Tristian's total acceptance of my bizarre life. Tristian had taken all that was wrong in my life and made everything bearable again. I was beginning to wonder if I loved Tristian for who he was as a person, or if gratitude, familiarity, and loyalty were playing a major part in my affection for him. I pushed those thoughts away from me, and concentrated on his enthusiasm of his friends' complete acceptance of me. Tristian's positivity emanated from him, and I couldn't help but feel the same, and match his grin.

We headed off in our separate directions, and I couldn't lie to myself that the joy I was feeling was totally a result of Tristian's infectious nature, but I was about to see Angel Xavier as well. I didn't think it was possible but when I got to my locker, Angel was casually leaning against it and my joy doubled if not tripled. I wasn't sure how I was going to keep Angel and I on a friendship level, but for Tristian's sake I had better find a way.

"Good morning Kikyo, I trust you slept well?" Angel had stepped away and opened my locker all in one swift movement that left me momentarily speechless. "Good morning . . . . How did you do that? Do you have my combination?" I was bemused by this small action, but not angry that he was able to open my locker. "Ah, Kikyo you are something, anyway, I was wondering if maybe we can talk over lunch about yesterday, but not in the cafeteria, how 'bout we meet in the balcony instead?" my heart pounded in my chest at the mere thought of being alone with him again that despite my better judgment, I agreed before I could really think on it. "Good, I'll get some lunch and meet you there." Angel's violet eyes bore into mine with such intensity that I was on the brink of actually swooning.

Angel Xavier and I walked into home room together, and all eyes were on us, I couldn't take my focus off of his violet eyes, and it's a wonder I didn't trip over my own two feet and fall on my face. Angel was speaking so low that I was sure only I heard him, or was it that he was inside of my head? No that was impossible. We took our seats and Mr. Kotwazinski, began to take roll call. I tore my gaze away from Angel and forced my attention on what Mr. Kotwazinski was saying about not forgetting to fill out the ballots for the Prom Court. I blushed when he read aloud (once again) the nominee's for prom king and queen, and the whole room went wild with a cacophony of cheers and applause. Angel gave me a private wink, and I was at ease with the atmosphere of the room.

It was strange, how Angel Xavier always put me at ease when he was around me. It was as if he could control my actions and emotions, as well as those of the people around us. It lead me to think that there was something more to Angel Xavier that I didn't know. I wanted to turn and ask him about it, when the bell rang and the thought hung in the air, unfinished and already dissipating. My questions would have to wait for lunch, but until then, I knew I would have to concentrate on Tristian or at the very least my classes.

I tried my best to listen in Math class, but my mind was not cooperating with me today, it was like if it wanted to focus on Angel Xavier and only him. No other thought or the day's lesson could break through the web of images that crowded my already fatigued mind. Angel and I had English together next, but I knew Mrs. Mertleman would not allow us to converse, besides we needed to talk about our Ibsen Project, so I had no choice but to wait for lunch to assault Angel with my many questions.

When the bell rang marking the end of math, I leapt from my seat and practically raced for English, not really watching where I was going, I almost smacked head-on into Angel Xavier. The huge grin that spread across Angel's face sent me into a red hot blush. I had to look away to avoid staring dumbly into his exquisite face and making a fool of myself. I let my loose hair cover my face, until I was able to control the blush that had spread over me with lightning speed.

Once I had control over myself, I turned to Angel Xavier, only to see him turned and speaking to the girl who sat behind him. She was blushing coyly and giggling at something he had said to her. I don't know why but it bothered me to see him getting that reaction out of this girl that neither one of us knew. Then I remembered that he actually might know her. He probably was friends with this girl back when he had attended this school back in my mental absence. I had to turn away before I gave my envy away and my face blushed again, only this time it would blush from jealousy and not embarrassment.

Thankfully, Mrs. Mertleman began the class, and I was able to concentrate on the lesson of the day. Hard as it was for me not to turn to look at Angel Xavier, I was able to force my attention on Mrs. Mertleman and keep it off of Angel. By the time the class was coming to an end, I must've been doodling unconsciously because I had drawn Angel's eyes all over the margins of my notes in my notebook. I quickly flipped the notebook shut, and stuffed it and my book, into my bag. Angel was once again talking to the girl whose name was a blank to me, and I quickly made my way out of class and headed for the ladies room to avoid my lunch "date" with Angel in the balcony. As the door to the ladies room shut behind me, I heard Angel shouting my name, from down the hall. There were a couple of girls at the sink, and with a smile in my direction they left me to myself. I locked myself in the handicap accessible stall, and buried my head in my hands.

I couldn't figure out why seeing Angel talking to that girl had sent me into this sudden burst of angry emotion. It shouldn't bother me to see him talk to other girls; after all, what was it to me? Angel Xavier was just my friend and nothing more. Right now, battling with myself over both Tristian and Angel Xavier led me to believe that I was much better off if I had stayed in my safe little bubble, at least until school was over for me and I could decide what was to become of me.

"Kikyo, come out of there are you ok?" It was Angel tapping on the stall door. Just hearing his voice echo off the tiles sent my heartbeat into overdrive. "What are you doing here; don't you realize this is the ladies room?" I didn't mean for it to come off as harsh as it did, but I had a very flimsy hold on my emotions at the moment, and I was lucky to be able to even get the words past my lips. "Kikyo, I know it's the ladies room, I've been waiting for you to come out for ten minutes now, so are you gonna come out, or am I gonna have to come in there and see what's wrong with you?" I didn't know what to say to that except to say, "Um, yeah, I'll be right out, um why don't you meet me in the balcony, and I'll be right there." "Not a chance, come on let's go, we need to talk." With a sigh, I gathered my things, put my emotions in check and exited the stall.

We walked in silence to the dark confines of the auditorium balcony. My anger and frustration had built up and escalated during that short silent walk. Once the balcony door had shut behind us, I turned to Angel Xavier to let him have it about practically dragging me out of the ladies room. I whirled around furiously searching the darkness for him, only to have my ire completely dissolve, as I stared wordlessly into his deep violet eyes set in his luminescent flawless face. For the moment, I couldn't even remember what I was about to say, and even less why I was so angry at him. My breath caught in my throat when he gathered my wrists in his icy cold hands.

"Kikyo, what was all that about? We had a lunch date, or did you forget?" His voice was pure honey, the sweetest melody my ears had ever heard. His eyes bore into mine, and seemed to read my every thought just like the last time we were here. "Kikyo, I'm finding it very hard to figure out exactly where we stand. I mean, one moment you tell me you only want to be friends and another you look at me with such intensity that I can't help but wonder if you don't want something else, and then today, I talk to someone other than you, and you get angry and run from me, so what is it? What is it that you want from me, is it "just friendship" or a deeper something?" I was dumbstruck, how was it possible that he could read me so well, could he see the turmoil on my face, I thought I had a pretty good mask of indifference going for me. I tried to lower my head or at least avert my gaze away from his, but it was like his eyes held me in place. I couldn't move.

I had so much to say, but no words would form on my lips. I wanted to tell him, how confused I was right now, I wanted to tell him, that he made me feel so much that I didn't understand, I also wanted to tell him that I ached to be with him, but couldn't hurt Tristian, my words failed me. What Angel Xavier said to me next, was a shock to my system; I couldn't comprehend what he was saying to me, or even how he knew what I was thinking. "Kikyo, please don't be confused, let your heart lead you, not your conscious, I know your experiencing things you don't even understand, and I know you don't want to hurt Tristian, but please, I can ease your ache if you'd just give me the chance." The look in his eyes broke my last resolve, and my silent tears spilled from my eyes, as I finally broke away from his firm grip, and turned my back to him.

I could still feel his eyes boring into my back, and when I whirled around, he was seated far down into the balcony, in the blink of an eye. How could this be, he was just right behind me. "Angel, will you explain this all to me?" the words were barely a whisper, which I don't even think I truly articulated. From across the balcony, I heard his unmistakable musical voice, as clear as if he were right beside me. "I will explain as much as I can, but not here, and not today." This was too much, my head was spinning, and I couldn't make sense of anything. I had to get out of here; I needed some fresh air to clear my head. "Kikyo, I think you should go and get some fresh air, go and clear your head, I'm gonna go, and sort some things out as well, I think I'll call it a day and go home or something." I couldn't even respond, I picked up my bag, and left as if in a trance.

I still had a few minutes before my next class began, so I went to my locker to kill some time. My head was so confused with what I had just experienced with Angel Xavier. I needed to sort things out, and wasn't sure I could even try to get through the rest of the day normally. I needed to get out of the presence of all the peering questioning eyes, but how could I do it without telling Tristian I was leaving? I didn't just want to disappear without an explanation, I could leave him a note taped to his locker, but what would I say? I could call him and let him know I didn't feel well and I went home on the bus. Either way Tristian would worry and skip practice to come to be with me. I needed to be alone, so I opted to call his cell and leave him a message; I went to the pay phone by the cafeteria and dialed his number.

"Tristian, its Kikyo, amor I'm not feeling well and I went home on the bus, don't worry I'm fine I just need to rest a bit. Go to practice and call me later, maybe you should have dinner with your family tonight, I'll see you in the morning. I love you." I hung up the phone with shaky guilty fingers and headed towards the city bus stop. I was fishing for my wallet to get change for the bus, when I realized, I hadn't taken the bus in so long, I didn't have enough change. Frustrated with myself, I began the long walk home, it was probably a good thing, I needed time to think anyway, and walking was good for me, since I hadn't ran in a long time either.

I got about three blocks from school, not really watching where I was going, just thinking about my difficult situation, when a car horn pulled me from my reverie and brought me back to earth. I turned towards the sound of the horn and saw it was Angel Xavier pushing the passenger door open for me. I got in without so much as a smile, just my same look of confusion still on my face. How did he possibly know where to find me? "Well, well what a coincidence, did you plan on walking all the way home?" thankfully. I was seated because his mere voice turned my knees to jelly. "Are you ditching? I thought it was just me, funny how things work out right?" I knew that if I turned to look him straight in the face, I would never get the words out, so I fiddled with my hair, and looked down at my lap, "Angel, we need to talk, but I think I need to think things through first, before I say or do something wrong. Can you do me a favor please, just drop me off at home, and once I sort out my jumbled thoughts, I'll talk to you and let you know where I stand on the "us" issue." I still couldn't look at him, I continued to focus my gaze on my lap, and the rest of the ride was silent. It took all of my self control to not look at him, his personal scent was so intense, I wanted nothing more than to embrace him tightly and inhale his scent until I was desensitized enough to not go into overdrive at his mere presence. I caught myself lifting my hand to reach out and grasp his in mine, like Tristian always did, but I stopped myself and ran my fingers through my hair instead and gazed out the window as my city changed from block to block.

With extremely minimal direction, Angel Xavier had found my block and was pulling up in front of my house, I thanked him for the ride and with a silent nod, and he reached over my lap to open my door for me. The close proximity was enough to break my resolve. My every nerve ending was abuzz with electrical charges, and my self control was finally bested. I stretched over into Angel's personal space and kissed his cheek. I silently slid out of the car, and sprinted up the stairs and into my house, never looking back.

I locked the door behind me, and slid onto the floor, my back to the wall. What had I just done? I wasn't sure but, either I was feverish from all the adrenaline pumping through me, or was Angel's cheek really so icy cold, just like his hands on my wrists earlier today? I needed to clear my head. I picked myself up off the floor and went to change into my running clothes. Tristian would be calling me for sure soon as he checked his phone, but I couldn't deal with him right now. I picked up my hair into a ponytail, laced up my sneakers, retrieved my i-Pod and was off.

Running in the daylight, was very different than running at three in the morning. I wasn't filled with the same sense of dread that consumed my every fiber when I ran in the early morning. It was a totally new world for me to see. I ran in my usual direction, flying past the houses and corner neighborhood convenience stores. The sun shone down on me and gave me hope for a better tomorrow. I ran towards my park, but instead of my usual pattern of running around its perimeter, I ran towards the center of the park, where the small manmade beach sat. The beach was deserted, so I headed for the garden instead.

The garden was beautiful; the park district must have already begun to plant the perennials, because most of the flowers were in full bloom. The garden was the setting for many a wedding and sweet fifteen photo op. I sat on one of the benches, and sorted through my jumbled thoughts. I had to weigh the pros & cons of each of my current points of interest. On the one hand I had Tristian who with his unwavering love for me, I could not stand to breathe if I was without him, but on the other, I had Angel Xavier who stirred every emotion in me that I didn't even know I possessed and made my very core tremble with excitement at the mere thought of him.

I laid on a bench and let the warm rays of the sun wash me in their light. I closed my eyes and conjured up every memory I had of Tristian. I started with our first meeting way back when we were just kids. I was so shy and small; Tristian immediately took the roll of my protector, and had been by my side ever since then up until my disgracing "episode". Tristian and I had a lifetime of moments and it was good that I could recall all those moments because he was my only connection to the world besides mom. Through Tristian, I learned it was ok to be different and shy, and because of Tristian, I learned to be strong. Tristian was an extension of me, my reason to breathe, and the only person who would truly mourn me if I were to ever fade away. My Tristian, my only "family", my love.

Angel Xavier, on the other hand, had no history with me. Yes I loved Tristian with every fiber I possessed, but Angel with his violet eyes, ruby lips, mysterious ways and magnetic pull was the polar opposite of Tristian. Angel stirred my senses, quickened my pulse and set my every nerve ending aflame. The attraction I had to Angel was not like the love I held for Tristian this was more complex, this attraction was even beyond sexual and sensual, this was on a level I had never experienced or even knew existed. What I felt for Angel Xavier was a sense that he needed me as much as I him. Between Angel and me there was something powerful that I could not explain, describe or understand. And even though I had just met this enigmatic being, I felt we had a history, we were connected in such a way that no words could describe. How to not hurt Tristian in the quest to find the answers I so needed was going to be extremely complicated.

My head was spinning with all the information I needed to sort through, I needed to get back home, I knew Tristian would be calling soon and if I didn't answer he'd be searching for me very soon. I lifted myself up from my comforting bench and headed home.

I walked back and enjoyed the sun engulfing me in warmth. I was feeling good and upbeat for once. With a smile on my face and a song on my lips, I followed my hard beaten path back home, for once not afraid and running for my life. I could feel I was on the verge of something big, some kind of epiphany or some life altering event that was looming just out my reach, but tantalizing enough that I could almost make it out.

When I got to my block, my stupor had not diminished at all, but once my house was before me, the familiar black clouds that engulfed my heart returned as if on cue. All the good feelings that accompanied me on the way home dissipated like a fine mist and were gone, only to be replaced by dread, despair, and darkness.

With my head down, and a sigh of acceptance, I ascended the stairs and entered my home.

I took off my ear buds, and placed them in my pocket, hung up my jacket, and was headed to the kitchen to prepare dinner, when a very familiar feeling overcame me. I felt the usual dread, as panic began to grip my every nerve. I stood frozen in place as the blood drained to my feet, and my eyes grew wide with the image they beheld.

A shadowy figure of a man stood under the arch between the living room and the dining room. For once I knew this was not a dream, not a hallucination, and not my imagination. The figure stood ram-rod straight with arms folded, cloaked in a long dark hooded robe, his face was covered, but I had no need to see his face, this was my attacker, my defiler, my nightmare come to life.

I stood rooted and as a million thoughts swam in my brain, no words could form on my lips. My head began to swoon, but I defiantly refused to give in to this monster and let him have me yet again. This time, I was prepared to fight him, or at least die fighting.

"Kikyo now is not the time, but I will be back for you, and you will be mine. You will be my bride, and you will do as I command" this he articulated not aloud but in my head. When I was about to respond, he was gone in the blink of an eye. The house itself gave me every indication that aside from me, it stood empty. I continued to stand and stare at the spot where he had stood for what seemed an eternity. The shrill ringing of the phone broke my stupor and forced me back to earth. I hadn't even realized I was shaking, not from cold but from the adrenaline rush that kept me upright.

I ran for the phone, and was surprisingly calm when I answered the phone. "Hello, Tristian querido" "Kikyo, are you ok? I got your message, but are you really ok? Do you need anything, can I do anything?" "Um yeah I'm fine now, I just wasn't feeling well earlier, um can you pick up some dinner tonight? I really don't feel much like cooking if you want to come over." "Sure amor, I'll get us something and be over after practice, see you then, I love you Kikyo" I hung up the phone and just knew something huge was looming in the future for me.

My afternoon had gone so well, I wondered why it needed to be ruined by that fiend that just couldn't stand to see me happy. I occupied myself with homework until Tristian came by, and even took a short nap. I awoke refreshed and not entirely sure that the events of this afternoon actually took place. I checked the time on the VCR and rushed about to be presentable enough for when Tristian arrived shortly.

Tristian arrived with dinner and we ate amongst light conversation of the supposed "headache" I had that made me leave school early. After much assurance that I was now fine, Tristian did some homework, and left for the night

I summoned all my will and took control of my body. I could tell from the thickness of the air that my assailant was wordlessly trying to control me. I felt pressure on my brain not like a headache but more like he was trying to pry into it; I felt an engulfing embrace as if he were trying to hold me in place, and I further felt his glare on me telling me with his eyes that this was his final victory over me.

The entire world seemed to pause, as the following events moved in slow motion. He silently unfolded his arms, and one bone white hand stretched out to beckon me to him as the other fell to his side. My will was too great and I stood my ground firm in my resolve to win this battle. When I did not comply with his wordless command, I felt every pressure point on my body pulsate with his power. I summoned a mental picture of my beloved Tristian, and gathered every last ounce of defiance in me to deter his powerful hold on me.

"Have you come to finish what you couldn't before?" the words came easy and fearless. My hands were fists of rage as my own nails dug into my palms. My fury was at its boiling point and I was ready to attack this monster, no matter the outcome. For once I would not be weak, frightened, or confused. "Why did you wait so long to finish me off, is it because now you know, I have a fighting chance, or because now I have a reason, no two reasons to fight back?" I was calmly addressing this monstrosity, still holding my ground. He was silent and immobile like a statue that exuded pure evil.

I broke free from my stance and crossed the room in an instant to snatch the hood off his head and see his face. I needed to see who he was and what he looked like, if for nothing other than to give myself peace and finally put a face to the fiend that had ruined my life. I knocked the hood back, only to see a face I never expected, like in my dreams, it was the face of my Tristian, at this my rage escalated and I pounded on his chest. It was like pounding on a cold marble statue, I could feel the icy chest through the thick robe, and when he gathered both my wrists in one hand, I knew this was the end of me. He lifted me off the ground a few inches as I kicked at the air. He brought me to his eye level, and turned the full power of his ruby, blood red rimmed eyes on me. He inhaled slowly, and I could feel my body give up my life force, I weakened more with every second that passed.

My body was limp in his one hand, but he kept my mind sharp. He wanted me to know what he was doing to me. I could feel his raw power wash over me, numbing my body and sending electrical shock waves through every fiber of my being. I wanted to scream but he seemed to be in control of my emotions as well as everything else. His eyes held mine, and I was powerless. I could feel my life energy draining from me, it felt like gentle suckling all over my body, a soft suction that was not totally uncomfortable; again, I tried with all my might to struggle and break free, but to no avail. He needn't even speak to me aloud, he was in my head, and that was where he seemed to want to belong.

When I felt the draining sensation wash over me one last time, he released his hold over me and I crumpled to the floor. My head swam with images of memories long forgotten, some of which were not my own. I could feel every emotion he ever felt in all his years. I was drained, woozy, and so confused as so many images vied for recognition in my weary mind. I felt him lift me oh so gently and crush me to him as he carried me to my room and laid me on my plush bed. I didn't feel angry, or frightened, or even confused anymore. I floated off to sleep on an emotionless wave and slept, dreamlessly and soundly.

In my sleeping state I didn't dream, it was more like memories of events from his Angel Xavier's life intertwined with memories of my pitiful life with Tristian. I compared the two lives I could have with either love. I knew to my core that a life with Angel would be filled with adventure, romance, epic love, but with all that also came, endless loss of life, forever losing my beloved Tristian to the eternal life I would choose, just to be in the arms of Angel Xavier for all time.

I was torn as I also weighed the life I could have with Tristian, we would grow old together, watch as our children grew and had children of their own. There was no denying we would have a gratifying life. I would fulfill all of Tristian's hopes and dreams, as he would mine. Tristian awoke me from the dark fog that clouded my life for so long, and to turn my back on him now would be just too devastating for both of us. He would give up everything humanly possible to protect me and be with me, but could I return the favor?

I awoke the next morning for once with a clear head, I knew what my mission in life was, and I needed to talk to talk to Tristian in order to say my final good-bye's to him. I couldn't leave with Angel Xavier without the closure I needed from Tristian. Graduation was only a few weeks away, I had made a silent promise to mom that I would graduate for her, only for her as my pathetic life had no meaning to me. I would talk to Angel Xavier and tell him of my decision to join him for eternity as his dark bride. We would go far from this place and leave behind my home for the beauty and brilliance of the world over. After graduation I would say good bye to life and hello to death and that life everlasting.

Angel would mold me and guide me to being a powerful Vampire; never again would I be weak and lifeless. He would set a spark in me that would grow to a full blown flame and once and for all Kikyo the meek will be a ghost of the past. Together we would hunt the monster of my dreams and bring him to his eternal demise, both Angel and I believed, the fiend would target Tristian just because he knew of his importance to me.

Chapter Eight

Research

"Tristian, we have to talk, can you come over?" I hung up the phone before I would even allow him to answer but I knew he would come. I dressed and began the hot water for a cup of tea when he was entering through the kitchen, worry written plainly on his face.

"Kikyo, as usual you had me so worried what's going on with you?" he ran his fingers through his hair in exasperation and sighed. "I don't know what to expect from you day to day anymore, you've changed. Kikyo amor I love you, but you're making it extremely difficult to know how you feel about me." "Well, Tristian that's why I called you over, like I said we need to talk . . . Tea?" I poured us each a cup of tea and followed him to the living room.

I was calm, cool and controlled. I knew what I had to say and do but for once in my life I was confident and ready to end it all once and for all with my beloved Tristian. I handed him his tea and sat beside him. I took his hands in mine and took a deep breath.

"Amor, you know I love you to death and you know I would never do anything to intentionally hurt you, but I think for both our sakes, it's time we both moved on. I will be eternally grateful for all you have ever done for me and my mom throughout all these years, but it's time you move on, forget about me, you have so much to live for and honestly I will only hold you back." I held my fingers to his lips to stop his protest and continued, "I know this will hurt, but only for a while as we both know time heals all wounds. Well not mine that so damaged me, but you will heal, your strong, beautiful and full of life. Tristian amor, we both know what happened to me and even if it is impossible to believe it's true. I can't subject you to this any longer. I love you too much and in order for me to protect you, I need to let you go."

"Kikyo what the hell are you saying? You're breaking up with me? You love me but you're breaking up with me; tell me how this makes sense? Does this have anything to do with Angel Xavier? I've seen the way he looks at you, it's like only you exist to him and the whole world be damned!" Tristian was visibly shaking and I could see the anger rising up in him like it always did in his father. I couldn't hurt this sweet innocent soul anymore. My mind was made up, and if I was going to leave this world for the next I had to sever all ties with Tristian. Against all my love and adoration for this boy, I was going to crush his heart and make him not want me anymore.

"Tristian, I know the full truth about what happened to me in the basement so many years ago, Angel Xavier told me everything, shhh my love let me speak. It was Angel Xavier who rescued me from the true monster who tried to destroy me; it was because of Angel Xavier that I am alive today. He stopped his maker from killing me, I was almost drained to the point of death when he battled for my life, his maker fled before he could end him and was severely injured, so much so that he needed to go underground since then just to recover, but in order to completely destroy him, I need to help Angel, but my love, I will need to be with him. I'm leaving you and this life to find him and kill him. I won't see you ever again, but if Angel is right once that monster emerges, he will seek you out to destroy you in order to hurt me. I can't let this happen. Your chance for a long life is the most important to me."

Tristian went pale and still shivered from his fury, his eyes full of hurt and loathing startled me, but I held my ground. His rage wasn't directed at me but at the monster, Angel Xavier, and the situation, I had never seen him like this, Tristian was the mirror image of his father when he was on a rampage. He stood above me, flung the tea across the room shattering the cup and saucer, then fell to his knees at my feet. Tristian held me so tight. He cried onto my lap and all I could do was slip back into my bubble, if I was emotionally unavailable, it wouldn't hurt me so to see the pain I've caused my Tristian. I consoled him as much as I could in my emotionless state and never once shed a tear.

"Angel is one of them? Angel's a Vampire? Kikyo how am I supposed to process this? You're breaking up with me, to be with a Vampire, for my protection? None of this makes sense! I knew there was something about Angel Xavier but this, Kikyo no; I can't let you be with him, this isn't real, it can't be real, Kikyo say it isn't so, say you love me and only me, well go away, anywhere you want."

I arose and lifted Tristian to his feet and led him behind me to my room. His protests fell silent as realization set in, I owed it not only to Tristian but to myself as well to *be* with him, to feel him move within me and have one last human experience that Angel Xavier could never give me. Silently I kissed him and prevented him from stopping me or saying a word, I undressed and stood before him and let him take me in, I wanted him to remember me like this, wanting him to love me, hold me and make love to me. My last human hurrah. The flames of passion consumed us both as our hands and lips found our every sweet crevice and we stroked, suckled, and burned to memory every second of our goodbye. We gave ourselves to each other completely and honestly without any remorse or embarrassment. My final gift to Tristian was my virtue and eternal love. Both of us spent we slept for hours and when I awoke I made coffee, dressed and left him sleeping in my bed as I went for a run, thinking of Angel Xavier.

My mind was made-up. In order to save Tristian from the inevitable death that Angel Xavier or his kind wanted to inflict upon him, I needed to be on the side of the eternal darkness, so that Tristian would be forever safe. I would vow to look-out for him, his mother and eventually his own family once he married and had kids of his own. He had given up his boyhood for me, now was my time to repay all his goodness. So I had made up my mind, at first I would have gone to Tristian and told him of my plan to be a "Dark Bride", but I knew deep down he would never allow it. I had to think of a new different permanent solution, what if I went to Angel Xavier and had him work it out so that I would have a public accidental death? Maybe I would be just another casualty of the mean streets of Chicago's inner city, just one more innocent life claimed by the vast corruption of the gang-filled nights.

I needed to have Angel Xavier prepare a place for us. Now that I was going to be a willing player in the theatrics of my own demise, I had to get everything in order. We needed to secure a home away from here. Away from anyone who had ever laid eyes on either of us. We needed furnishings and money, I wasn't exactly sure how Angel lived or how he came by funding, but I was willing to do whatever it took to keep Tristian safe. Tristan's life and happiness was all that mattered at this point. So I knew that Angel Xavier needed to understand that I wasn't going to consent until after graduation, and I would be adamant that until then I would spend every last second available with my beloved Tristian until my public expiration.

My head was spinning with all the ideas running through it. Was it possible that I had actually found meaning to my life, only to have it short lived and snuffed-out as quickly as I had come to its realization? No matter, my mind was made-up. If that God-Forsaken monster was to come after me again, I would be ready this time, I would have the power of strength, knowledge and purpose on my side to finally once and for all defeat him. Tristian need never know of the ugly shadows that lurk in the night. I was flying on a natural high as I made a checklist of what I had and what I needed in order to make this transition as smooth as possible, but I did need to be clear as to what I needed to do for my transformation. I wasn't even sure if all I knew from movies and books was real for a vampire, again I had to consult with Angel Xavier. My body was abuzz with all the excitement, not necessarily happiness although to spend an eternity with Angel was something to look forward to, but also a deep sadness to have to leave my beloved behind.

When I got home, Tristian was still sleeping. I showered and began breakfast, when I carried a tray of food to my room for us; I saw that Tristian was gone. He left silently without a word, only leaving a two word note on my pillow. "Gotta think" I understood, but that didn't lessen the hurt.

I dialed Angel Xavier with shaky fingers, "Angel, we need to talk, can you get here quickly?" I didn't even wait for an answer. I disconnected the line and put water to boil for some tea. The water wasn't even hot when Angel stood before me with arms outstretched waiting to envelope me. He was like a magnet that I was drawn to. I held him tight, and inhaled his special scent, as I ran my still trembling fingers through his loose hair. It took all my will to release him and step away. "Angel . . . um I have questions and have been going over things, so . . . here goes . . ." I couldn't look at him directly for fear of losing myself in his eyes; I instead looked down at my steaming cup of tea, and felt his eyes read my every thought.

"Ok . . . Angel, first of all I have to set some ground rules, there will be NO prying into my thoughts or memories, and also this is something I'm choosing so understand what I'm saying before getting upset . . ." at this the melodic sound of his voice gave me goose bumps, "I understand my love, I will wait until your done then I will speak". "OK, good . . . now Angel I have decided that this world is just much too dangerous for me to be in it as I am, so I have decided to join you as your bride and be rid of this place. But I do have conditions of course. First I need details based on fact not on what humans are led to believe. For my transformation, what do I need to do in order to prepare? What I mean is, and I know it may sound dumb, but it's important to me, like if I cut my hair and nails now, will they never grow back once I'm like you?

If I were to say cut myself later would I bleed and scar or would it just magically heal and leave no trace? Will my scars disappear? Is it a necessity to drink human blood? Can you eat or drink anything if so how does it digest? And I'm sure there are lots more questions, but let's start with these." Angel Xavier chuckled at me, and took my hands from across the table, "Oh my Kikyo, you do amuse me so, but before I answer any of your questions, let me just say that you have made me the happiest man . . . dead or alive . . . on earth. But I'm sure that this decision was not an easy one, and I know there are stipulations as well, but we'll get to that soon enough. Now as for your questions, yes I would need to prepare you, forget all you have ever read or seen about my kind. Contrary to popular belief, we do not stay young always; we do grow older but just not as quickly as humans. We do sleep, but not in coffins, we can eat and it is absorbed into our blood but it is uncomfortable and slows us down. Everyone's Dark Gift is different, for instance I can read thoughts but you may not. We do grow stronger as time passes and we do have incredible strength, speed, agility, and cunning.

It's not necessary to drink human blood, but that keeps us the strongest, for those of us who do not like to kill our prey, we can take the life force of humans, it drains them like an alcoholic binge but if we know when to stop, they will just sleep for a while, and we can live off of that, but we need it more often than blood. You can cut your hair and nails now, but it will take centuries to grow them back to their length now. And as for your scars, they will diminish and with time disappear. If your injured once you've turned, you will heal quickly depending on the severity of the injury, we can be shot and stabbed, and we'll heal instantaneously but if you sever any appendage, you will not grow it back. If you burn or are beheaded that is instant death. Oh and sunlight, it can be uncomfortable if exposed for a long period of time, but we can learn tolerate it. But one necessity is the contacts, the reason my eyes are violet is because they are red, and to counter you can wear dark lenses, but I choose the blue for a violet color. So did I answer all your questions?"

I blush at the truth of it and despite the flush in my cheeks, I press on. I need to have all the facts before I give in, this will be one decision in my life that I will never be able to change once the deed is done. The unspeakable monster that destroyed my life has to pay for what he's done, not only to me physically or psychologically, but for ending my path before it even begun. Armed with the new knowledge of what was before me, I steeled my spine and let the last vestiges in me that were complacent, idle and frightened die and fall behind me.

"One last thing . . . I need distance from you for now. I will be with Tristian if he'll still have me for the remainder of my human life. I have "given" myself to Tristian, and I will continue to do so until my death. I don't think this is too much to ask, since I'm giving you my eternity. I don't want jealousy or interference from you, yes keep us safe, but give me my time with Tristian." Of course Angel agreed, and gave me a final embrace before vanishing from my arms, leaving a whisper in my ear vowing his love.

The new Kikyo was about to emerge from the ashes of that protective bubble that had housed me for so long, I was to arise like a phoenix with a vengeance that no one would expect, least of all my foe. Tristian would one day come to forgive for leaving him without a word, without an explanation, or even a chance to allow him to attempt to change my mind. He would one day have to forgive me for allowing him to continue to live, to study, gain a career, date, marry and have children and grandchildren. Tristian would one day understand that my leaving was all for him. Maybe one day in his old age I'll come to him and explain it all . . . Maybe.

After Angel Xavier left, I was too wired. I called my boss and explained that I wouldn't be coming back to work, I thanked him for all he had done for my mom and I, he understood and told me to call him if I ever wanted to come back. I went about and did my mundane chores, finished clearing out mom's room, and the remainder of any school work due before graduation was completed in a couple of weeks. I was almost ready.

I changed into my running clothes and shoes, took a look at the time, and chuckled to myself that it was once again three a.m. what a coincidence. As I had done so many times in the past, I put on my headphones and locked the front door. I had a purpose for once. I ran towards the park, never looking back, never locking eyes with the permanent sentry but most importantly, locking out the panic and uncertainty. I knew deep down that even though Angel had left, he was still watching me, keeping me safe but allowing me the false comfort of independence. I knew in that instant that all I ever wanted would be given freely through Angel Xavier, not only monetary items, or physical goods, but knowledge and unconditional love.

My head was clear; my thoughts raced a mile a minute almost as fast as my feet over the pavement. I flew over the cracked concrete of the sidewalks, past the usual buildings, cars, storefronts, and undesirables. I ran without a care for I knew now that all I had to do was put forth all my effort in learning everything that Angel had to teach me before that abominable monstrosity gained enough strength to come for me full force, by then I would be ready for him. I'd have my new Vampire strength, knowledge, and insight to defeat him once and for all. All the wasted years I spent in that bubble were about to be redeemed. I had read all the vampire based novellas and seen all the movies, but none of that was even a whisper at the truth that I was about to embark on. This was real, not a book or a movie. The glamor was enticing, but even that from what I gathered from Angel was incomparable. I hungered for my face off. I needed to make amends with my wasted life. Tristian deserved better than I could ever give him. Tristian would suffer for me no longer.

On agile feet I soared. I circled the park in record time, as if the devil himself was clawing at my dust. I was exhilarated with this newfound passion. The blood raced through my veins hot and spiked with adrenaline. By the time I reached home, a huge weight had been lifted from my overburdened shoulders. I showered, and let the hot water relax me and calm my rapid beating heart. If I was to survive this, I needed to be ready for the unexpected. I will from this moment forward expect to see HIM lurking in a shadow or peering at me from a distance, I would allow HIM to penetrate my mind no longer. I knew he prided himself on the weakness he created in me, but I was no longer weak. The most powerful thing I now possessed was the fight in me. I was giddy with the anticipation. Angel Xavier and I would have to prepare my body for the transformation. I was thinking maybe a waxing, a manicure and pedicure, a trim to my uneven ends? I knew this was all very girly and something I had never done aside from the trim, but it was necessary for the new me. For once in my life I was going to embrace life. I didn't know when Angel wanted to change me, but I had every intention to *live* life until then.

Chapter Nine

The Beginning of the End

It was nearly noon, and I still hadn't heard from Tristian, I recalled our night together, how our bodies molded into one. I had taken control and explored his body as much as he did mine. I gave myself to him completely without any remorse or embarrassment. My emotions commanded my every fiber. I had never been so close to Tristian as last night. We were a fluid tangle of arms and legs that moved as one to that ultimate euphoric state, that we achieved repeatedly all night until dehydration and exhaustion overcame us.

During our lovemaking Tristian kept trying to change my mind, but for his own good and against all my common sense, all I could give Tristian was the purest love that I could ever give to anyone. I truly felt that with this show of unmarred love, he could come to someday understand that I loved him too much to stay with him.

I wondered if he would come back, or if I that was the last time he and I would be together or even speak. I wasn't completely oblivious to what went on at school, and I knew that prom was this coming week on Saturday, but Tristian never even mentioned it to me. I wondered if I should call him and find out if he wanted to go, things like this were important to Tristian and I wanted to do something special for him.

As I dialed Tristan's house, an irking feeling crept into me and I began to wonder if he would even take my call. I did want a clean break, but not yet, not after cramming what life I had left into these next two weeks. The phone rang, once, twice, three times, I was about to hang up when Tristian answered a little out of breath. "Kikyo, I said I need time to think, please don't contact me, I'll find you when I'm ready." The line went dead before I could even utter a word. I was crushed. I let the phone fall to the ground as I slid down the wall in shock. Did my Tristian just blow me off? Really . . . did this just happen? This was not part of my master plan. As hard as I knew it would be I had to give Tristian time. I owed it to him; I owed him so much more so what was a little time?

Since my last conversation with Angel Xavier, I had been thinking about the shape that the new "Me" would take. I had no intentions of ever blending into my environment like I had done for all my life. 95% of all my clothing was black or neutral, color had no place in my life. Tristian had always loved me regardless of my wardrobe, but now I was ready for a huge change. I was going to take notes from all the horror B-Movies I had ever watched with mom. I wanted to embrace my new life with open arms. I wondered if the Goth look would befit me.

I didn't have anything to do since I had told Angel I wanted to spend my last days with Tristian, and now with Tristian blowing me off, I was alone. I began to think of what life would be like with Angel Xavier my soon to be eternal companion. He would teach me, train me and mold me to be a strong Vampire. I would have no fear, no remorse, no nightmares, and no more wasted life. After graduation, I will say goodbye to Kikyo Starlita Aoki Martinez, the freak and say hello to Kikyo Garcia San Salvador, the fearless take no prisoners Dark Princess on a mission.

I began to think of mom and how she would've insisted I go to prom, she probably would've even set me up with Tristian saying something like it's a rite of passage and since I didn't allow her to make me a Quincenera, it's like a sweet 16 but for Mexicans it's done at 15. I wore a simple white dress that belonged to mom and we went to church then out to lunch. I guess since I would never get to marry I could at least do this in memory of mom. I needed a dress, I myself didn't have anything in my closet that would be acceptable, so I needed to raid mom's closet maybe just maybe she had something I could wear to snap a picture in and keep as a memento of what I left behind.

I had forgotten about when Tristian and I had cleaned out mom's room and donated most of her belongings to charity. I was a little bummed that I didn't have a dress for prom . . . or a date for that matter, I guess I could always go with Angel Xavier, but how would I ask him? I would have to call him in the morning and see if he would be a willing partner. I guess it was for the best that Tristian and I go back to where we were before my emergence from the bubble. I hadn't asked Angel about memories, like would they fade after the change or would I retain vague fragments of this pathetic life I led. Maybe it would be best to forget it all and let my new life create its own memories. Either way, I should document this life before it all fades away to nothingness.

I had a journal I use to keep back when I was younger, so I figured I could add to that one. Mom had given me a keepsake box that my dad had given to her, it was old and from dad's family passed down to all the generations. All that ever was of Hiro Aoki and Rosario Martinez would die with me, the last living blood relative of both those lines, never to procreate and carry on the line they produced. I had some old pictures of dad, mom & their families, my journal, a few pieces of jewelry, and old coins from both sides. With the addition of a few recent memoirs I would cherish the contents of that box for all eternity. I didn't have any recent pictures of Tristian so I would have to clip them from the yearbook once it's passed out. I would also throw in the police report just to remind myself one day that in some lifetime I was human and had a family of my own.

Through tears, sobs, and heartache I wrote in that journal until my hands cramped, the sun rose, and realized I had written volumes, there were only a few pages left in that book. I realized it was ironic that the few pages left would be enough to document my last few memories before my end. I was famished but since I was writing all night in the same cross legged position on the floor, my legs were asleep and I could move very fast. I unknotted myself from the floor and put my memory box away in the closet.

I needed sleep, food, and to seriously empty my bladder. When I came out the bathroom, I felt uneasy, like once again I wasn't alone in this house. I needed to call Angel Xavier; I wanted to ask him to prom anyway. I was two steps out the bathroom, when he was sauntering into the kitchen with the biggest, sweetest grin. "Kikyo, I would love to be your date for prom, who know we may even be crowned King & Queen", he kissed the top of my head like Tristian would have done, as he bear hugged me, ever cautious to not crush me. I was still stunned, as I nervously chuckled and pushed him off of me. "No fair, you're not supposed to listen to my thoughts, but I forgive you, and yes I want you to be my date, except now I need a dress and you need a suit oh and we have to buy the tickets, so I guess since I'm inviting I get to buy the tickets." We both laughed lightly. "Kikyo why don't you go change and I'll make you breakfast; besides I have a surprise for you."

I threw on some jeans and an oversized pullover, twisted my hair into a pony tail and stepped into my sneakers. I could smell the food cooking and the coffee brewing. I took a seat in the kitchen as Angel served me a plate and slid the buttered toast across the table to me. I smiled between delicious bites as Angel prattled on about everywhere we would go, and everything we would see and do. He cleaned up after I was at the busting point, and told me to go sit in the living room while he fetched my surprise. I did as I was told and before I could even sit, he was back with a large garment bag and an even larger smile on those perfect kissable ruby red lips.

"For my prom queen" he said as he unzipped the bag and took out the dress I would wear to prom. It was perfect for the occasion, kinda like Goth Princess meets Quincenera. It was black with sequins, lace and a leather corset. The shoes beautiful patent leather platform pumps. If I ever wanted to make a statement, this was the dress to do it in. A nice up do and maybe red carnations in my hair should complete the look. Most of my scars had faded so I was sure the dress, the hair, and some intense makeup would be just what I needed for that wow factor that would leave all the wagging tongues in awe. The rest of the days following up to Prom night, consisted of Tristian avoiding me and Angel Xavier filling me in on Vampire Lore.

Prom was tomorrow, and Graduation was next week. All assignments and finals were turned in and completed. It seemed as if everything in my life was coming to its finale, just as I was getting ready to embark on my new life. I was like a caterpillar in its warm comfy cocoon ready to emerge as a beautiful carefree butterfly. I was ready to soar and fly & with Angel Xavier by my side, I will finally be free of this lonely existence that was my life. Angel would give me hope, information, and most of all the strength and confidence I had always lacked.

Angel came over a few hours before prom and helped me do my hair, and get me ready for the ultimate event of my human life. When we were done, I took a look at myself in the full length mirror and couldn't even recognize myself, I was beyond stunning, so much so I couldn't stop staring at myself. If only Tristian had not closed me out, I would be going with him to prom, but it was for the best, we needed the distance for when I completely vanished from his life.

Angel and I arrived at the prom venue in style, a nice sleek black limo with tinted windows, champagne and chocolate covered strawberries. The prom theme was "Red Carpet Hollywood" complete with a red carpet, paparazzi-like photographers, and the under classmen cheering us on, snapping pictures and handing over yearbooks for our signatures. I was actually having fun. I was unrecognizable at first, but then when they all noticed who I really was, the excitement shot up astronomically. By the time we entered the venue and were at the top of the stairs, all eyes were on us.

I found Tristian in the crowd and looked him in the eyes, I said nothing but so much was said with just one look. He averted his eyes and excused himself from his date and rushed out, Angel gently squeezed my hand and led me down the stairs. Classmates hugged us hello throughout the night as we danced, took pictures, and enjoyed our night. The cherry on top was being crowned King & Queen, after the royal court was called, Tristian and his date Elizabeth were part of our court. Tristian would not look at me, talk to me or stand anywhere near me. I felt bad but I was determined to enjoy this. Angel made sure I was happy all night, and when it was time to go, I had Angel go to flag down the limo as I ran back to our table, where I had left my purse.

Tristian was quick to take advantage of the opportunity. He took me by the arm and led me to a quiet dark corner, where he crushed me to him, and kissed me with such a hunger, that all reason left me momentarily. I came to my senses when Tristian was ripped from my embrace with such a force that I was thrown down on the soft sofa that caught my fall. Angel Xavier and my beloved Tristian were about to exchange blows when I found my voice and shouted for them to stop, they both let go and as Tristian's eye was swelling, the bruise on Angel's cheek evaporated. I saw the blood on Tristian's lip and wanted so much to hold him and make it all better but I knew I couldn't I had to get Angel away as quick as possible. I took Angel by the arm and tugged him away, mouthing "I'm sorry" to Tristian.

We drove away, and Angel apologized for his behavior. I told him I understood, and that I forgave him, but he should've known better. I couldn't wait for graduation to be over so that I could finally put this life to rest. Why did this life have to be so complicated, when did my life take this path? With all the questions swirling around my mind a mile a minute, I didn't even realize were were at my house so fast. Angel was still immaculate and there were no signs of the bruised cheek. I was at ease again once I looked into those violet eyes and that sense of peace and calm washed over me.

Angel helped me out of my dress and loosened the pins out of my hair letting it fall in long waves down my neck, back and shoulders. He traced the line from my jaw to my collarbone with light kisses. He lifted me to him and held me tight enough for me not to fall. I knew then that our life together would be filled with uncompromising understanding and unconditional love. He laid me on my bed and kissed me goodnight. Angel Xavier, ever the gentleman sent me to my dreams leaving me images of the magical night as he saw it.

When I awoke the next morning, Angel was gone. My dress was gone and I feared Tristian was gone from me too. Angel left me a note on my nightstand, written in his calligraphic handwriting saying, he took my dress and his suit to the cleaners, and was also going to run some errands, he'd be back later tonight and there was a surprise on the dining room table for me. I got up to collect my surprise and stepped on flower petals, not red roses like in the movies, but red carnations, like the one I wore in my hair. The petals led me to the dining room where a huge bouquet of red carnations rested in a black vase which almost resembled my dress. On the card written in Tristian's sloppy boy writing was, "If forever turns out to be too long, I'll always be here for you . . . all my love Tristian".

I hadn't realized I was crying until my tee shirt was wet with tears, and my bladder was screaming for my attention. I showered, dressed, ate and busied myself with chores and errands. I surfed the internet for any and all information I could find on vampires from movies to novels to vampire culture. Comparing to everything that Angel Xavier had told me, all this information seemed comical and childish. What I was dealing with was real. From the information I had gathered through Angel's teachings, the whole myth of crucifixes, garlic, wooden steaks, coffins, bats & holy water, were just that . . . myths. According to Angel, sunlight didn't kill a vampire, it did however debilitate. The sun acts like acid so it's no wonder vampires hid in the dark, not only for the comfort level but also to stalk prey. After some time a vampire could build a tolerance to the UV rays and one day walk in the sunlight.

Blood unfortunately was a necessity. Human blood kept a vampire at his or her strongest; it was the ultimate food source. Animal blood was comparable to a light unfilling, low-fat zero calorie snack. A human's life source was used not so much as a food source but as a way to gain knowledge from the prey. The mind reading, super strength, rapid movement & stealth are all gained through time and strengthened with blood.

I was lost in all the information I was cross referencing, that I didn't even hear when Angel Xavier came in. He came over to me and kissed me hello as I was shutting down my laptop. Angel held the garment bag with my cleaned dress in one hand and handed me my yearbook with the other. "Your surprise I promised, Kikyo". He went to my room to hang the dress in my closet as I thumbed the yearbook, signed by what seemed to be the entire graduating class of my high school and the faculty. It really was a nice surprise, this book would have to go into the memory box and now I wouldn't have to cut out the pictures of my beloved Tristian. I was ready for this new life and graduation couldn't get here fast enough. The last week was filled with graduation preparations and practices. Angel had already secured a remote location for us somewhere far from Tristian. According to Angel Xavier, I will be in a blood rage for about a week, before I can even begin to control myself. Once I can master self-control, Angel will wean me from my initial diet of undesirable human blood, to animal and human blood then once I have a good handle on my consumption, I would go strictly animal, after he taught me to fight and we defeated the fiend of my nightmares. This was my plan and when I told Angel about it he laughed at me and said he'd support me in whatever I chose to feed on.

I hadn't spoken to Tristian since the scuffle at prom and even that didn't constitute as a conversation, I had to speak to him, if only to say my goodbyes to him. I was a nervous wreck standing in the hall, wearing my cap and gown, not nervous because of the graduation, but because I knew this would be my last human act. Tristian was way ahead of me in the processional as we were lined up according to last name and Angel Xavier was like twenty behind me. The auditorium was filled with parents, loved ones and bright futures, only Angel and I had no one to congratulate us as we accepted our diplomas and left high school behind.

One by one all my classmates were called, they went up the stairs, shook hands with faculty, accepted their diplomas, posed for a picture and returned to their seats until everyone was called. My thoughts were scattered and only came together when I heard our Principal call "Mr. Tristian Garcia Jr." as he walked up to the stage all his academic and athletic achievements were accounted. When he accepted his diploma and posed for his photo the auditorium erupted in a cacophony of cheers, whistles and applause. He found my eyes and held them for a second, as a tear escaped my eye.

More names were called, and when it was my turn, I stood on shaky legs. I ascended the stairs, shook hands, accepted my diploma, and posed for my picture. It seemed like an eternity but as time stood still, I found my Tristian with tears in his eyes, quickly found Angel Xavier and saw the rage in his violet eyes as he bore daggers into Tristian. I left the stage and let out a breath I didn't know I held until I sat back down. All my other classmates paraded up on stage as well. Angel Xavier was met with cheers and an outpouring of love comparable to Tristian's. Once we had all been called, we all stood and transferred our tassels from left to right. Everyone snapped off the tassel and caps were tossed into the air.

It happened so fast I didn't realize it was happening at all. I saw Tristian lunge at Angel Xavier over mingling classmates. Chairs were tossed aside, bodies moved out of the way, and the scuffle that began at prom continued here at graduation. I couldn't hear what was being grunted between them, but I knew Angel was holding every ounce of strength he had back. Tristian summoned all the fight he had in him to attack Angel. I could almost feel when he shattered his fist on Angels jaw. Angel shoved Tristian only hard enough to send him summersaulting over some chairs and tripping over a group of hugging girls.

I got to them as if in slow motion and stood between them, just as faculty pulled them each away. Tristian kept screaming at Angel that he wouldn't allow it, over and over as he was carried out. I took Angel Xavier and pulled him out a side door before this got any worse. Despite Tristian's display of macho-ness, I still love him so much that in order to ensure his longevity, I had to walk away tonight. The fiend was hurt and currently recuperating and if Angel and I were going to defeat him, I needed to turn immediately, Angel said it would take a few months for him to come after me and my beloved and his mom as they were my only loved ones, the fiend would come for them, if I didn't go quietly, he'd probably finish them either way just to spite me. There wasn't much time left. I begged Angel for a few minutes so that I could give Tristian a proper farewell.

I ran to find Tristian, as once again Angel went for the car. My poor Tristian still had a healing eye from prom, his fist was shattered, his lips were swelling and I felt as awful as he looked. "Tristian mi amor, why did you do this, you know I love you, I'm doing this for you. I know you don't understand this now, but one day I'll come back and I'll explain everything to you. My love, please know that all I want from you is for you to be happy. Please live your life to its fullest and never have a doubt about my love for you. Amor I have to go, I don't know when I'll see you again, but I will be back again someday. Just remember that the girl in the bubble you rescued long ago will always be right here in your heart, I'll never be more than a thought away. Tristian I've made my choice, and you know what it is, please don't come after me. All you ever wanted was my love . . . Tristian; you've had that since before we were born, and will have it long after we're gone.

Crimson Fog:
Chasing Dusk

Coming Soon…

Acknowledgements:

Thank You to my wonderful family and friends for supporting me through the production of my life's work.

Raffie, Cesar, Evelyn, Mom, Pops, Pr. Hector, Pr. Jade, Sofia, Maria, the Berrios's, all my countless friends from way back and most recent, and all the Wonderful patient understanding & awesome people at iUniverse!